Carrie's Story

by

Molly Weatherfield

CLEIS
PRESS

Published in the United States by Cleis Press Inc.,
P.O. Box 14684, San Francisco, California 94114.
Printed in the United States.
Cover design: Scott Idleman
Book design: Karen Quigg
Cleis Press logo art: Juana Alicia
First Cleis Press Edition
10

Carrie's Story

This story about a readerly-writerly girl
is dedicated to my readerly-writerly girlfriends
and, always and already and of course,
to my husband.

Passion and expression are not really separable. Passion comes to birth in that powerful impetus of the mind which also brings language into existence. So soon as passion goes beyond instinct and becomes truly itself, it tends to self-description, either in order to justify or intensify its being, or else simply in order to keep *going*.

—DENIS DE ROUGEMENT, *Love in the Western World*

Contents

Preface

I WROTE THIS S/M ODYSSEY OF A VERY YOUNG, very intellectual girl in the early 1990s, but its roots go back about a dozen years earlier, when a friend had asked me if I was going to a Take Back the Night March. Those of us who date back to the feminism of the late 1970s will remember those women's marches through urban red-light districts to demonstrate against pornography. Something about these marches disturbed me, but until that moment I hadn't known why.

"No," I told my friend. No, I wouldn't march.

"Why?" she asked.

I stammered a few unimpeachable sentiments about the First Amendment, but I knew I wasn't being completely honest.

"It's because of who I was when I was younger," I finally said. "In my teens and early twenties. I read a lot of S/M porn back then before feminism."

Lots of Sade anyway. *Story of O*—innumerable times—as well as the inferior imitations it had inspired. I hadn't been hurt by these books. I'd read them bravely and honestly, helplessly and joyfully, deep into the night. Blissfully enthralled by narrative, my younger self hadn't bothered to sort out sex from intellect, power from creativity. I hadn't thought about it for years, but I knew I couldn't participate in a movement that wanted to "protect" other women from the confusing pleasures I'd experienced.

The more I thought about this conversation, the more I wanted to reach back to the young person I'd been. I wanted to reconnect with her fledgling sexuality, and to find out how she'd come to be so smart (especially since I knew that she'd considered herself exceedingly stupid). Over the years I'd learned something about politics and literary theory, but my younger, porn-reading self had understood stories and their seductive power directly.

Of course, reconnecting with the erotics of reading and writing wasn't something I undertook alone. No member of the boomer generation ever does anything alone. I had only to look around me: what came to be called the Sex Wars were raging within the women's movement throughout the 1980s. Feminists debated pornography and censorship. More importantly, we thought long and hard about the relationship of sexual expression to action, nature to culture. I read and listened, learning invaluable lessons from the boldest (and sometimes most beleaguered) fighters for "pro-sex feminism," notably Susie Bright, Gayle Rubin, and Amber Hollibaugh.

I learned even more from the feminist pornography that was suddenly, deliciously available. This new stuff tried to democratize the old conventions of bondage and domination and absolutely refused to be complicit with anybody's victimization. Of course, with the important exception of Anne Rice, feminist pornography was largely created by lesbian, gay, and bisexual authors, written with all the *brio* of a movement creating its public voice. I'm a straight married lady, but I nonetheless treasured the first Samois collection, and I devoured the work of Pat Califia, Carol Queen, and John Preston.

In some ways, it was like revisiting the heavy hetero French porn I'd read so many years ago. But in other ways, this late twentieth-century porn bore the indelible marks of its own era. Confident, optimistic, flush with the wisdom of consciousness-raising and a new grassroots "sexpertise," this porn believed in consensual relationships, fulfillment, and happy endings.

As I gratefully do as well. Except that on another, private channel, I kept hearing the older stories. "Chateau porn," my husband called it. Well, that was part of it; I've always been a sucker for the moment when the heavy double doors shut behind you and there you are, bound and gagged and alone with your terror and desire.

I wanted more attention paid to the very strangeness of that moment: the deadpan humor implicit in all the chatty, philosophical storytelling that flows out of a gagged and bound O or Justine. Perhaps I'd simply read too many French writers: God help me, I wanted a little more theory. How *did* mind and body conspire to produce these stories anyway? Perhaps I'd find out only by telling one myself.

I'm grateful to Richard Kasak, who thought that people would want to read such a thing, for the original Masquerade edition. Many thanks to Felice Newman for making this Cleis edition possible. And my deepest thanks go to Darlene Pagano, for convincing me—at a time when I needed a lot of convincing—that people might still want to read *Carrie's Story*.

Molly Weatherfield
San Francisco
May 2002

CHAPTER I

Jonathan

I had been Jonathan's slave for about a year when he told me he wanted to sell me at an auction. I wasn't in any condition to respond when he told me this—I was very carefully licking his balls, concentrating on doing it the way he liked, wondering when it would be time to snake my tongue into his asshole, waiting for the little tug on the chain clipped to my nipples, which would be the signal. I got it right, I think—or at least close enough. His cock got very big, and he rammed it deep into my throat, coming hugely, while he continued to tug on the chain. I swallowed hard, letting myself sigh and shudder. He held my head down tightly with one of his hands, only very slowly releasing it, allowing me to relax between his thighs.

It was only later, after I had brought in some tea and buttered toast and knelt silently at his feet while he read through the book review sections—*New York Times* and *San Francisco Chronicle* both—occasionally stroking my head and feeding me bits of toast with his fingers, that he decided to tell me what he had meant.

"Did you hear me before, Carrie?" he asked.

"Yes, Jonathan," I said, following the rules we maintained. I always had to address him by name, and deferentially. I also had to look him straight in the eye, which I was doing as well. "But I didn't understand what you meant," I added.

"Well, get dressed," he said. "We'll go for a walk, and I'll tell you."

"Yes, Jonathan," I said. He removed the nipple clips and attached a leather leash to the collar around my neck. The leash dangled down between my breasts, and he pulled it up between my legs, looping it around my waist and knotting it in the back. He often said that he wished he could take me on a leash whenever we went out, but he couldn't without causing a stir. So this would have to do. The leather felt tight between the lips of my cunt. I put on a pair of jeans, a big turtleneck sweater, and some high-heeled boots. You couldn't see the leash or collar, of course, but I was very conscious of them, as I always was. Jonathan had gotten dressed while I was getting the tea, but I helped him put on his boots and got his leather jacket from the closet.

We looked, I guess, like any yuppie couple out walking on Filbert Street on a Sunday afternoon. No, to tell you the truth, we're better-looking. Or at least Jonathan is. He has warm olive skin, a lively, quirky, intelligent face, and very bright brown eyes. He's tallish, with elegant shoulders and a tapering waist. I'm not as special-looking, though I think I'm okay, and I do think we look nice together. His gray hair and brown eyes look great against my brown hair and gray eyes, and we have almost matching very short haircuts. As for the rest of me—a little taller than average, small bones, slender hips. Pale skin and a wide mouth. Stormy gray shadows around my eyes, even when I've gotten lots of sleep.

The day was a little foggy, but we were warm from sex and tea, and I was too confused and curious to worry about any chill in the air anyway. Jonathan held my hand tightly and began to explain.

"You don't know about the auctions, I guess," he said, "or how slave ownership really works. But haven't you wondered, when we've gone to dressage shows, what the real relationships are?"

"Yes, Jonathan," I said meekly, "I had hoped you'd tell me."

The dressage shows were among the stranger events Jonathan had taken me to. They had their rules, too. They'd take place in some very fancy house, really a mansion, usually down the peninsula, often with walled grounds you'd drive through on the way to the house. Jonathan would give the car to a valet, who would also take my coat. Without my coat, I'd be naked, except for boots and a leash and collar. Jonathan would take my leash and lead me to the chairs set up in a ring, usually in some gorgeous garden area. He'd take a seat and attach the leash to a little post set up next to it, and I'd kneel there, as all the other slaves were doing next to their little posts.

The first couple of times we'd gone to these events, I couldn't entirely believe it. I mean, I wouldn't have been surprised if Jonathan had just hired this bunch of attractive people from central casting, that's about how real it was to me. It was hard for me to believe, or admit, that other people were participating in arrangements similar to the one I had with Jonathan and that, moreover, there was a world of them — a miniworld, anyway. But little by little I began to accept at least a certain level of factual reality. Physical facts, like the thin red lines on that blond, curly-haired girl's thighs. They were precisely spaced, those lines, and I had to believe that they were the work of that very sallow, soignée woman in white silk whom the blond girl was gazing at so adoringly. I had accepted the evidence by now, and I was

3

beginning to wonder how much more there was to all of this and how it all worked.

Jonathan had had no patience for my curiosity. The point of the show, he'd told me in no uncertain terms, was the performances. I was there to watch and learn from them, not to drool over the audience. Or, to be more precise, the point for me should be those performances he was interested in. Because actually there were many kinds of performances featured, including races and steeplechases performed by slaves in boots and harnesses, sometimes in color-coordinated equipage (were there really people who had more than one slave? I wondered). Jonathan didn't care so much about the horsier parts, though, and sometimes left early. As I followed him out I'd be filled with disturbing feelings, incoherent imaginings, for example, of what it would feel like to be commanded by tugs at reins attached to a bit in my mouth.

What Jonathan did care about, though, were the performances called presentations. These were likely to be up at the front of the program right after the introductions, which were usually delivered by some very manicured rich man or lady. Last time we'd been to one of these, it had been a lady in a garden-party dress, welcoming the assemblage to her home, in a creamy voice. Then she announced the participants, although actually that information was all on a beautifully printed little card, which had been distributed to all the masters and mistresses when they'd come in.

Anyhow, her announcement had gone something like, "Today, we have six lovely participants in our first event. They are Elizabeth, owned by Mr. Elias Johnstone; Janet, owned by Mr. Frank Murphy; Tina, certifiably owned by Mr. John Rudner…" and so on. Six naked, very beautiful young women walked twice around the ring, then each in turn kneeled before the lady and kissed her foot. Each of them had her name, the name of her master, and some other code numbers that I didn't understand elegantly stenciled in grease pencil at the small of her back. The garden-party lady smiled at all of them and then introduced the judge, who, it seemed from the audience reaction, was very well known, for whatever it was he usually did. Maybe it was this. I overheard some whispering about his working wonders as a trainer, whatever that was, with somebody's slaves. Anyway, he had a great body and a not so great haircut. He was wearing a sort of Jack LaLanne getup. And he got a lot of applause.

The performance itself was very simple and very difficult. There were formal positions, called presentations, that the slaves had to strike in turn. These were sexual positions, of complete compliance and availability. There were, as you might imagine, a mouth position, a cunt position, an ass position, and variations on all these. The idea was to strike a posture in which you would be most easily and appealingly fuckable. It had a lot to do with muscle control. Even if you weren't the judge, who would put the slaves through their paces and try them out, you could see that there were right and wrong ways to do it.

I particularly remembered the slave named Elizabeth, who I thought was really good. She was wearing a very high collar, which seemed to be made of silver, but which was probably stainless-steel mesh, like a good, flexible watchband. She had dark hair, tied in a small knot on top of her head like a ballerina, and big, guileless, pale blue eyes, outlined in black. Her only adornments were a pair of bright nipple clamps, probably also of stainless steel, and a white orchid attached to the side of her head. Her breasts were large and firm, and her waist and ribcage were very small and delicate.

The trainer held a small whip, which he mostly used for pointing and gesturing. He pointed to her and said, shortly but calmly, "Elizabeth. Mouth." Slowly, and with wonderful grace, she kneeled in front of him, holding her body so her mouth was perfectly in line to receive his cock. Since his pants were on, I don't know how she judged the probable angle of his erection, but she put her open mouth six inches from his crotch, arching in a perfect curve from the small of her back to her neck, so that when he unzipped his fly, there she was, to the naked eye immobile as she received his cock down her throat and began to suck. You could tell, too, that her throat was wide open and relaxed and that she was breathing gently through her nose. Her eyes were wide open and serene. There was scattered applause.

The trainer didn't keep his cock there for long, of course. He pulled it out, very large and very erect, and said, "Elizabeth. Cunt." This looked especially difficult to me, as there was nothing but the soft grass for Elizabeth to lie on, but she didn't lie down—rather, she stood on her toes and levered herself slowly onto his cock, until he was all the way in, and then she wrapped one arm around his shoulders, a little like a trapeze artist sliding down the rope. "Elizabeth. Ass," he continued, and she levered herself off and got down on her hands and knees. You could see, somehow, that her ass was beautifully open, though still hot, tight, and young. Her face was meek, beautiful, impassive, but somehow lustful. There was more applause as he quickly got in deep, then pulled out and stroked her head. She turned around, kissed his foot, and then kissed the ground in front of the audience.

There was quite a bit of applause, and then Elizabeth got to her feet and returned to the circle. I was very taken and tried to file away my impressions for later use.

In fact, though, Elizabeth didn't win first prize. She came in second. Tina, certifiably owned by John Rudner, came in first. I wasn't sure why, but I figured that I still had a lot to learn. Still, Jonathan was impressed with Elizabeth, too, and went over to talk to her master during the champagne break. I saw Elizabeth shyly kissing his foot, and then he shook her master's hand and stroked her breast. The red second-place ribbon was pinned to her collar. I, of course, was still kneeling with all the other tethered slaves. Next to me was an absolutely gorgeous boy, all shoulders, suntan, cheekbones, and flowing hair. He whispered to me, "Your master is fabulous-looking. Are you certifiably owned?" I had no idea what to say, but didn't have the chance anyway, as one of the servants who was setting out little troughs of water for us to lap from came over and slapped the boy for talking out of turn. Then another one came by with a bucket of SPF30 sunscreen and started slathering me with it, rubbing it in hard, and finding ways to get in some invisible but painful prods and pinches.

In any case, as Jonathan was explaining to me now, what "certifiably owned"—which Tina had been and Elizabeth hadn't—meant was that Tina had been bought by her master, probably at an auction. This didn't clarify things a whole lot for me, but it was a start.

"Well, in that case, Jonathan, am I just plain 'owned' by you?" I asked.

"No," he answered, "not even that. This is just an informal arrangement. I want to formalize it, though, so that I can sell you."

"Will you make a lot of money if you sell me?" I asked. The words felt so strange in my mouth that I forgot to call him "Jonathan."

"You'll get ten strokes when we get home," he replied, and then calmly continued, "No, that's not how it works, not in this century. If you formally give ownership of yourself to me, then we'll draw up papers and I'll own you and I can sell you. But I get a pretty nominal fee. You actually get the money — it's held for you in trust and earns interest until your term of service ends. Terms of service are usually a year or two."

I was silent, partly because I was thinking of the ten strokes. But this was also a lot to digest.

"How much money, Jonathan?" I asked.

"Tina," he said, "cost her master $250,000 for two years. Let's go home."

When we got back to the house, I helped him off with his leather jacket and hung it up. Jonathan sat down in his armchair, and I came and stood before him, trembling. I hoped he'd forget about the ten strokes. I knew he wouldn't. "You know what you have to do," he said quietly. "Don't dawdle."

"Yes, Jonathan," I said. I dropped to my knees, pulled off my sweater, boots, and jeans, and folded them as quickly as I could. I crawled quickly to the closet, put them away, and then crawled to a cabinet, where I got his rattan cane. The cane made me tremble more as I crawled back to him. He took the cane from me and removed the leash, unhooking it from my collar and deftly unknotting it from around my waist.

"Over the table," he said. There was a small table near his chair. I stood and bent over it, folding my hands at the small of my back. He stood up, grabbed both my wrists with his left hand—hard—and pulled them up in the air behind me. Good, I wouldn't have to worry about keeping them out of the way of the cane. And his holding my wrists like that would help me keep my balance, too. All I had to do was bear the pain and count the blows. And then it was really happening. God, it hurt. I kept it together, more or less, just sort of whimpering until the fourth stroke, when I gave in to the pain, sobbing and crying even as I called out each stroke by number. Before the tenth stroke, he shoved his foot between my legs, kicking them open a little, so the last stroke hit right where my pubic lips began in the back. I think I screamed before I remembered to say "ten."

He let go of my wrists and I slid to my knees again. He shoved the cane in my mouth and I crawled to put it away. Then I crawled back and knelt in front of him, thanking him and promising to try to keep the rules better in the future, and he held my head in his hands and kissed me lingeringly on the lips and on my cheeks, which were cold and wet with tears. He bent his head down and kissed my breasts, too, while I let out the last little volley of sobs. "Crawl out to the kitchen," he whispered. "I'll see you later."

In the kitchen, Mrs. Branden gave me my dinner in a pan on the floor. And after I'd finished eating, she led me upstairs to Jonathan's bedroom, where I waited on the bed on my hands and knees, my collar chained to the headboard. I figured that Jonathan had probably gone out to grab some dinner, maybe a beer, with friends. I knew I'd have to wait at least an hour, but, well, waiting's part of what I do. Amazingly to me, I usually stay in position, even when nobody's watching. When he came in, he snapped his fingers. I lowered my face to the pillow and folded my hands at the back of my neck. My back arched, and I became open, relaxed, ready.

He stroked the back of my head, reached under my shoulders, and caressed a breast. "Good, Carrie," he said. I murmured my thanks. I was really happy, in fact, no longer to be in disgrace. My ass hurt a lot—it felt huge and swollen—but in a funny way this didn't feel entirely bad. I felt, well, *there*, open and available. No question about there being a there there. I knew exactly where there was.

Jonathan fingered my ass thoughtfully, making me whimper, then stroked his tongue along one or two of the longer welts. I began to moan. He got up. I could hear him in the bathroom, peeing, washing, and brushing his teeth. Then he came back into the bedroom and got undressed, slowly and carefully putting his clothes away and whistling a theme from the "Trout Quintet." He liked anticipating pleasure; I'm an antsy, impatient kind of person, but I'd learned to see what he got out of the stately way he paced these things. Trembling on the bed, with my face in the pillow, working to contain my sighs and moans, I couldn't see him, but I could hear little things—the closet door turning on its hinge, a zipper sliding open, clothing rustling, the tiny sighing sound that was the squeeze of the Charlie's Sunshine bottle—all behind the sad, sweet melody he was cheerfully whistling.

Finally, naked, smelling of toothpaste and oatmeal soap, he climbed behind me. He whistled a rousing final bit of Schubert—he'd been doing both the strings and the piano—and then he entered me quickly. Did I say I was ready? I was almost ready, I guess. But for me there's still always that shock, that invasion, that readjustment, it felt, of everything, including—especially—my will. And then that moment of reacquaintance with the smaller sensations, the pure little pleasures, the feel of the sweetness of his belly, the fine black hair on it, the muscles stretched across his pelvis, perfectly curved around my painful butt. He took his time, fucking me slowly, luxuriously, up the ass. Floating, buffeted by waves of sensation, I tried to anchor myself to something besides the pleasure and agony by kissing and nibbling at his hand, planted on the bed next to my face.

Afterward he sleepily unhooked my collar and cuffs, while I bowed my head and thanked him. He sent me to my little bedroom at the end of the hall. I fell asleep confusedly trying to sort out all this owning, buying, and selling business and the flood of feelings it had loosened in me.

I woke up early the next morning and tried to hurry out to work. I supposed that Jonathan was still asleep—he's an architect and owns his own company, and some mornings he doesn't go in until 9:30 or so. It's better that way the mornings I'm there—I mean neither of us really wants to run into the other one when we're trying to pull ourselves together for a day at work. We're pretty cool about it, but it's hard to know how to act when we pass each other in the hall. So I'm glad he can leave late some mornings, because I work as a bike messenger downtown and I sure can't.

Like most mornings, I pulled on black tights, torn, baggy khaki pants cut off below the knee, neon orange Converse high-tops, and a ratty brown leather bomber jacket, with a T-shirt underneath that said DEAD ELVIS. I was achy and groggy, which was slowing me down and threatening to make me late, but I was also starving. Jonathan's refrigerator usually had good food in it—sometimes I wondered whether somebody was thinking about what I needed to eat for breakfast, doing physical work as I do, or whether Jonathan just normally liked to eat well. I sometimes made myself huge cheese omelettes before taking off in the morning, but today there was no time for that. So I hoped I'd find some cold pizza or something. I opened the refrigerator and—paydirt!—there was half a carton of Mu Shu pork. No pancakes, but you couldn't have everything. I wolfed it down out of the carton and was out the door.

Mostly, I like my job. I like being loud, fast, tough, and rude, and buzzing traffic and peds on my bicycle. Today, however, it wasn't so great, what with my sore ass. And I was still distracted by vague thoughts of auctions, ownership, and money, losing my edge and damn near getting killed by one of those bozos who open their car doors while you're zooming up beside them.

I hadn't really planned on being a bike messenger, though. I'd sort of assumed I'd be going to graduate school in literature when I met Jonathan during my senior year at Cal, at a party in a fancy house in Pacific Heights.

The party wasn't my kind of scene at all. It was given by a rich lawyer who seemed to know film people. I was there because my roommate Jan wanted to be a filmmaker and was sniffing at the outside of that scene. We'd gone to a movie in the city and run into some people she barely knew, and they brought us along to the party. It was the kind of party you feel self-conscious at if you're dressed as I was—black jeans and a Mime Troupe tank top. It was a rare warm San Francisco night in October. Women were wearing fantastic silky floaty-looking things, and men were looking very pulled-together, very *GQ* in Armani jackets. Jan seemed to be having a good time with the film people. I got a beer and drifted around, feeling shy.

They were showing videos in one of the rooms, on a huge high-resolution screen, so I wandered in and sat on the floor, figuring that this would keep me from feeling too lonely and at loose ends. I caught the last fifteen or twenty minutes of *Tribulation 99*, which was wonderfully funny and made me glad, for the first time, that I had come to this party. Then somebody put on an S/M film. It was awful, clearly playing for camp value. I gathered from the hoots and conversation attending it that somebody at the party had—when in desperate financial straits years ago—shot it or directed it or acted in it or something. It was about this dominatrix and her consort—the dominatrix is big, bleached, and blowsy, and has huge breasts with hefty rings piercing the nipples. And the guy—what do you call him, the dominator?—wears leather pants and no shirt and his skin is pitted from acne. Anyway, this cute lesbian couple comes to live with them because they aren't getting it on very well and need to be whipped into shape, which they are, and it does wonders for their sex life. It's all very trashy and inept, and the lesbian couple dissolves into giggles periodically. But I got into it.

Actually, it was very embarrassing that I got that deeply into it. I felt my cheeks get hot and I found myself staring and sweating a little and going slack jawed. Quickly I shook myself out of it, hoping nobody had noticed. The lights came on and I started out of the room, when Jonathan sort of materialized and fell into step beside me.

"They really are in that business, you know," he smiled charmingly. "I've met them."

13

"You mean Sir Jack and Mistress Anastasia?" I was proud that I could answer so calmly. "Are they good at what they do?"

"Actually, yes," he said. "They're not very glamorous, but, yes, they are good at what they do."

I had no idea what to say next, it suddenly occurring to me that I was talking about S/M with the most gorgeously Armani-ed man at the party. Thin, tan, intelligent-looking. Little black pearl stud in his ear. He wore the loose, elegant suit as though it were no big deal, and those wonderful, animal brown eyes were sexy, friendly, and cool enough to pretend he wasn't having to put me at ease.

Oh, my goodness, I thought. Wow. Middle, maybe late, thirties. Rich. Straight, or mostly so, anyway. And beautiful. I'd never said it before about a man, even to myself, but there it was, there *he* was. I felt gawky and somewhat sweaty. And tongue-tied. But I didn't take my eyes off him.

Which he had the good manners to accept as a compliment. And continued chatting, pleasantly and intelligently, not following up on Sir Jack and Mistress Anastasia. We went out to the balcony and sat on a stone balustrade overlooking the bay. And pretty soon I was telling him about school and literature and what I was actually interested in. Which was troubadour poetry, which got us talking about the south of France. He was smart and well read and he seemed to know everything about medieval architecture. Not that I really care a whole lot about medieval architecture, but I'm sure he'd picked up on how I'm an incredible sucker for expertise—of any kind, really, short of maybe earned run averages and runs batted in. I thought he was terrific— I mean, I was charmed and flattered and, face it, he was certainly the oldest and classiest person who had ever shown any romantic interest in me. I felt that maybe I actually liked him, too, but truthfully, I was so infatuated—and turned on, first by the porn movie and then by him—that I couldn't really tell and didn't entirely care. I wanted him to take me home with him, though. I knew that I cared a lot about that.

Until finally he put his hand on my arm and took a deep breath. Oh my god, he has AIDS or something, I thought wildly. But…

"Look," he said, "you're pretty and very bright and I like you, but that's not why I've been talking to you for the last hour. The thing is, I'm got something much more serious in mind. I want you to be my slave."

Oh. My. God. If I'd said it out loud I would have sounded like a refugee from "Beverly Hills 90210." Oh my god and *ee-yew*, gross. Talk about your conversation stoppers, I thought—this certainly gives a whole new meaning to what they call "meeting cute." I just stared for a minute while I carefully considered whether there was any chance I hadn't heard him correctly. But Jonathan has wonderful diction and it was quiet out there on the balcony and my hearing is just fine, so there was really no mistaking what he'd said. I slid off the balustrade and turned to go. "Uh, well, it's been nice talking to you," I stammered. Damn, he had seemed so fantastic, and it turns out he's just majorly sick. But it would make a great story. I could already imagine telling it.

"Hear me out," he said. He seemed so unflustered that I found myself stopping and turning to him again. "Look," he said again, patiently, "we were watching an outrageously tacky and stupid porn film in there and you could have mopped the floor with those jeans." His matter-of-fact gaze rested on my hips a heartbeat longer than it needed to, I thought.

15

"So," he continued, "I don't think you're nearly as shocked and scandalized as you'd like to think you are. After all, it's not as though you haven't thought about these things before. And at some length, I bet. In fact, my guess is that you've been jerking off to S/M porn since you found a copy of *Story of O* when you were a twelve-year-old baby-sitter. But I don't think you've ever done more than read and jerk off. Which is a shame. Because I think you'd be good at the real thing. I'm good at the real thing."

Thirteen and a half. Almost fourteen. I mean that's how old I actually had been when I found that copy of *Story of O*. Of course, that's typical of Jonathan's almost pathological politeness—one of the little things I learned from him is that it never hurts to give the other guy credit for a little more charm or precocity than he or she actually possesses. So probably he knew he was flattering me a little, in a perverse way, but he obviously also knew that, in all the ways that counted, he was dead-on right. S/M porn was one of my secrets. I didn't understand why I liked it, but I knew it was important to me. It seemed to occupy a space in my head next door to the more typical romantic passions—little-girl crushes on actors and rock stars and even some English teachers, the silly sweeping pleasure I always get reading *Jane Eyre*. And—Jonathan had made it so embarrassing—the romantic feelings I'd been having talking to him before the conversation had taken this disquieting turn. I felt very frightened and exposed.

But I had to say something. Enough about me, let's talk about you. "You got good at it hanging with Sir Jack and Mistress Anastasia?"

"I hang with a much better class of pervert. Well, they're richer, anyway, and they're a lot prettier. But you're right, in a

16

way. I do respect those silly-looking guys from the movie. It takes passion to act out your fantasy when you're going to look so graceless. I'm good at spotting passion — sincerity, maybe. I spotted *you*."

He reached into his pocket, found a piece of scrap paper, and scribbled his name and address on it — in predictably tiny, superlegible writing. "For a good time," he said, "come by, tomorrow at three." And then he wandered back into the party.

A star is born, I thought insanely, noticing that my jeans would mop up the whole terrace, at this point maybe the whole mansion.

And the next day at 3:00, reader, I went to his house. I didn't tell anybody about it and I'd even shaved my legs and under-arms. His house was a little unusual for San Francisco — brown shingle and set back from the street among ever-greens. I rang the doorbell, and he came to the door in jeans and a sweater. He was as friendly and charming as he'd been the night before, and he looked even better. He hadn't shaved, I realized. I guessed that this made us even, in some odd way, and I liked the way the stubble brought out lines and shadows around his mouth. Behind his pampered thirty-something look, there was just a touch of wildness. Yves Montand, I thought, in *The Wages of Fear*. The look contrasted with his calm, polite good humor. "I'm glad you're here. Come in."

He led me down the hall to a very beautiful book-lined study. There was a low fire burning in the fireplace, and he stood me in front of it. And very efficiently, neither of us saying a word, he took off my shirt and bra, helped me out of my jeans and underpants, took off my shoes and socks. He handed me a pair of very high-heeled shoes and told me to put them on and walk around until I got the feel of them. They fit pretty well, though I'd never worn anything nearly that high. Then he put a leather collar around my neck, buckling it in the back. He guided me by the shoulders, stood me near the fireplace again, and picked up the remote from a little table. He pressed a button on the remote, and a chain descended from the ceiling over my head. He put leather cuffs on my wrists and hooked them to the chain. Then he fiddled with the buttons on the remote again until the chain retracted back enough to be taut, and I was almost standing on my toes, hardly using the spike heels at all. Hardly breathing, either.

Jonathan sat down in a nearby armchair, leaned back, and surveyed me placidly. "I was right," he said. "You like this. Now answer my questions, and always address me as Jonathan when you do. And keep looking at me—no turning inward toward your own fantasy version of what's happening. No talking out of turn, either. You're here to tell me what I want to know. You can ask me questions later."

His questions were cold and clinical, though of course enunciated with the most careful civility. Age, height, weight. My family. Schedule and time obligations. Diseases, allergies. Sexual experience, in minute detail. He even scribbled down a few notes. It was hard to take a breath and find my voice, to keep looking at him, to remember to use his name. The fire was warm at my back, but I had to fight to keep off the shakes.

"Turn around," he said, finally. "I want to see your ass."

This was tough, given the shoes and the tautness of the chain. But—"Yes, Jonathan"—I did it. He leaned over and grabbed me—thumb up my ass, middle finger up my cunt, and held me as though I were some yard goods he was considering buying. He used the other hand to trace the shape of my buttocks. I could feel their roundness below and the two dimples above, as though he had drawn a picture for me. I thought of buying grapefruit at a supermarket. All the images that flashed through my mind, in fact, were of buying things.

Keeping hold of me, he used the hand that had been fondling me to slap me, hard. I gasped. What had I done to make him do that? I opened my eyes and looked around to see what he was doing. But he didn't respond, except to hold me a little tighter with those fingers that were up me. Mostly he was just looking at the spot he'd hit, at the bright pink color, I guessed. It seemed to me he liked the way it looked, and I realized that this had very little to do with me, or who I usually thought of as "me." This had to do with the texture of my skin, the shape and heft of my flesh. I had been right when I'd flashed on supermarkets and such. He was shopping. And god help me, I wanted him to want to buy.

Well, I thought, he had, after all, used the word "slave" out there on the balcony. But, you know, I'd thought of it differently then, more as in "slave of love" or something equally silly. I hadn't thought of him seriously inspecting, evaluating the merchandise. My face, and most of the rest of me I guess, flushed deeply, and I started to weep with humiliation. I was horribly embarrassed to be exposed as silly, shallow—missing meanings that should have been clear as day. Mostly, though, there was the obvious humiliation of being chained, helpless, open, obvious. Not only was I doing this, I was mortified to realize, but I was unmistakably turned on by doing this, soaking wet inside, in fact, and of course he could feel it. And I didn't even know if he cared one way or another.

19

Finally he let go of my ass and turned me back around. Then just leaned back and watched me cry, as though that were interesting, too.

When I'd calmed down a bit, he asked quietly, "Do you like to be looked at?"

"Yes, Jonathan, I do," I sniffled, but I was surprised by the certainty that underlay my weepy voice.

"Good," he said, and pressed the button to loosen the chain.

"On your knees," he continued, "but keep your back straight up and down and your chin up. That's a position I like." He pinched my nipples, hard, and he slapped my breasts.

"Have you ever been whipped or beaten?" he asked.

"No, Jonathan," I said.

"You will be," he said. "Enough to leave marks but not enough to scar or break the skin or injure you in any other way."

He pulled off his belt, doubled it, and stroked my breasts with it. He traced the outline of my mouth with it, and the smell of the soft leather was overwhelming. I drifted off into the sensations I was feeling, my eyes closing, and began to moan.

"Quiet," he said sternly, and then, "Get back here and pay attention." I opened my eyes wide, startled by the new tone in his voice. He looked at me for an instant and then continued in his polite, somewhat pedantic mode, "That's the sort of thing you'll learn not to do. I'll teach you. I have canes and whips. You can trust me to give you just a little more pain than you think you can stand. I'll beat you if you break the rules or for any lapses in form or sensibility, and sometimes I'll just do it for fun."

"Now," he continued, freeing my hands, "crawl over to the other side of the room and make sure you keep your ass high in the air. Pick up that rattan cane from the chair over there in your mouth and crawl back over here to give it to me. And don't slobber over it."

"Yes, Jonathan," I said, and did it. The cane was about thirty inches long, just a flexible reed that was a little thicker on the end he reached for when I came back. He told me to kneel up again and to put my hand out.

"This is the most painful thing I'll use," he said, "and only to punish you. So I want you to know what it feels like. It's what they used in all those famous brutal faggy English boys' schools."

It really did whistle through the air and it really did hurt like hell, raising an angry livid welt immediately. I gasped again, but this time I held back the tears. I can't keep from crying if he hits me again, I thought. But I didn't think he would. After all, the point of this blow was to communicate, not to punish. It was to introduce me to the currency we'd be dealing in. At least that's what he'd said, and I realized that I believed him. I guessed that was a good sign. Still, I realized that, while precise, his message was also intentionally and profoundly ambiguous, because I knew that he wouldn't tell me how many of such blows I'd be receiving.

"Get dressed," he told me now, "and sit down over there. Do you want some coffee?"

I nodded.

He spoke into an intercom. "Mrs. Branden, could we have a pot of coffee, please? Thanks."

Mrs. Branden? I hurried to get dressed and sat down in a straight chair nearby. He picked up the remote and retracted the chain back into the ceiling. Thank God. I hadn't thought

I could concentrate on talking to him with it swinging ever so slightly, a few feet from where I was sitting.

"Okay." He smiled. "Now, let's make a deal. But first, ask me anything, everything. Address me any way you want. If you sign on, you won't get this chance very often."

A pleasant-looking woman in her late forties came into the room. She wore a tweedy sweater and skirt and some artsy jewelry, and she carried coffee and cookies on a tray. She looked like a hip legal secretary, I thought. "Hi, Carrie." She smiled.

"Hi," I managed, and she smiled again and left.

Jonathan poured coffee. "Mrs. Branden's my housekeeper. And yes, she knows exactly what's going on. It's okay, though."

I turned to him in fury. "What do you mean it's okay? I thought we were alone," I sputtered.

He offered me a cup of black coffee. I nodded and took it. And he laughed a little. "That, you've got to get used to. You will, though. This is pornotopia—it's a place, Carrie, a place where people live like this all the time. This afternoon and all the times we'll spend together in the future are normal here. Normal depends on strict and absolute rules that everybody agrees on ahead of time, and it also means that it's not a big hush-hush thing. There are witnesses. That's part of the point and the pleasure. Total environment, or at least a convincing facsimile. Virtual reality."

I tried to think fast, but my mind felt dull and sluggish. So I swallowed some coffee and took a deep breath.

"Wait a minute," I said. "Let me get this straight. Mrs. Branden works for you. She knows what you do in here. She thinks it's okay."

"Do you think it's okay?" he asked.

I had to consider that one. "I don't know," I stammered. "I do know that it scares me a whole lot. I mean, well, I mean... I mean, I don't really know whether something that can make me feel so...so...make me feel like I feel right now...could really be okay. The only thing I know for sure is that I want it. Maybe I'll just have to wait to find out whether I think it's okay." I was astonished to hear myself say that I wanted it, but I knew it was true.

He nodded. "That's fair," he said, "and brave. And smart, too. But then, that's partly why I want you, because you're smart."

He seemed to specialize in this sort of friendly, matter-of-fact remark, lobbing them into the conversation like grenades aimed at demolishing every bit of cool I had left. I didn't know what to say next. What were we talking about, anyway. Oh, yeah...

"So, Mrs. Branden," I said. "Is she into it? Does she like it?"

"How would I know?" he said, laughing. He had a sur-prisingly pleasant, ordinary laugh. "I've never asked her. I haven't got the slightest idea. I pay her a lot and we're very nice and friendly with each other. It would be a whole lot harder for me to keep all the rules I like to keep without her. Listen, Carrie, I can see that Mrs. Branden was a shock to you, but don't you want to know anything else?"

"Okay," I said, "tell me some of these rules you keep around here."

"You are always here when you say you'll be here. With school, what would you say that means? Two weekday evenings, late Saturday afternoon through midday Sunday? I won't take more time than a boyfriend. Less, probably. You come to the side door. Mrs. Branden lets you into the kitchen. You undress, and she puts on your leash and collar and whatever else I want you to wear. She leads you in here. You're tethered and waiting at attention for me when I come in. And then you do absolutely everything I say. That's the easy part."

"That's disingenuous," I said, trying to hide my discomfort and, yes, my excitement. Tethered and waiting...

"You're right," he said. "It's not easy at all. But I think it'll be worth it for you. I'm a very responsible, methodical person. Stuffy, when you get right down to it, but the good side of that is that I'm consistent, detail-oriented, and very dependable. It's a good deal, really—you do everything I say, and you get a lot, quite a lot, of what you want."

"How do you know what I want?" I asked.

"Well, it doesn't take a rocket scientist," he said. "I mean, you're here, aren't you?"

I nodded grimly.

"Sorry," he smiled, "that was a cheap shot."

"But I do know what you want," he continued, "in essence if not yet in all its particulars. I can recognize it in your eyes and in your open mouth. You do like to be looked at: admired or belittled, adored or punished. You want to be *done to,* by a desire that's more selfish and specific than your own. You want that blank, floating moment of release, of submission, of knowing that it's useless to resist. Free fall, happening faster than even a motormouth like you can describe it.

"And you'll put up with the trite details, the silly redundancy of what we'll do, because I'll be showing you ways to capture that moment, again and again and again. I'll give it narrative shape, I'll keep it going, I'll figure out the particulars as we go along. And I'll stay ahead of you. You won't have to worry about that."

The fire hissed just then, and one of the logs fell over, punctuating what he'd said with a little flourish and fanfare of sparks. I sat stock-still, trying my damnedest to believe that this was really happening. I rubbed the painful welt on my hand, glad to be reminded of corporeal reality. I looked at him hard and he looked back serenely. He knew he had me.

I shuddered, but realized that I was also nodding my assent. Still, I wasn't ready to stop questioning him. "And suppose I call it all off," I said.

"Hey," he shrugged, "you know my address. I'll give you my phone number. I don't have yours and that's fine. I don't need it. So you can end this thing whenever — and however — you want. Write me a letter. Or you can call me up anytime and tell me you're not coming anymore. You can leave a message on my machine. Fax me, e-mail me, whatever. Or you can simply never show up again. But when you do come," he continued, "you'd better be prompt."

He pulled a card out of his pocket, very businesslike now, and rummaged around the table until he found an envelope. "Here's my doctor's card. Make an appointment for an HIV test. Get a complete checkup, too. I'll pay. And here's a copy of my latest HIV test. You can verify it with him. You can see one from me every month."

"So you get tested every month," I said. "Suppose I start fucking somebody else?"

"You won't," he said.

I was amazed. "That's an outrageous thing to say. Why not? I mean, you know how attractive you are, but that doesn't mean I won't fuck somebody else."

"That's not the point," he said. "I'm very glad you think I'm attractive, but that's not what I'm talking about. You won't fuck anybody else — at least, not on your own time — because you'll be too aching, exhausted, and fucked out to want to try. Trust me." I did, too, though I wasn't crazy about this obnoxious *quien es más macho* little speech. Still, his delivery was impressive, casual and understated, as though he were ordering a burrito. "Just a little more pain than you think you can stand, please. With onions and hot sauce."

He pulled out some more cards from his pocket. "And get a haircut. Like mine, really short, maybe even shorter. Very butch, only it won't look butch. It'll look...well, you'll see. Anyway, they'll know what I want. Oh, and a leg waxing, too."

"You pay for that kind of stuff too? Regularly?" I asked.

"Yeah," he said. "I'm rich, or rich enough, anyway. And I know pretty much what I want, and I've spent a lot of time figuring out how to get it. When you're rich, price isn't important. The main point is getting things to be the way you want them. So I pay. Your job is to work that beautiful butt off to be as perfect as the scenery around you. Oh, speaking of scenery. You know, if this works out, we could go to Provence."

"No!" I shouted, before I was even aware that I was saying anything.

We were both surprised. "What I mean is," I stammered, "Provence is a real, historical place, not a fucking virtual reality. And it's a place I care about and want to learn about and understand. And when I go there, I go as me, wearing my glasses and my own clunky shoes. It has nothing to do with this."

26

The ironic lines around his mouth deepened. "Rio maybe, then."

"Maybe," I said.

It took about two weeks to get all the arrangements made—the doctor, the haircut, all that. Nobody in the expensive, tasteful places he sent me to seemed to think it was weird when I asked them to bill Jonathan, though I found it humiliating in the extreme. They had to know, I kept thinking, these polite and urbane functionaries. And certainly, the haircutter did seem to know exactly what Jonathan wanted, and no, it didn't exactly make me look butch. When he finished, I stared at myself for a long while in the elegant chromed mirror. I looked terrific, actually, in a cold, high-tech sort of way. Jonathan must have a great eye, I thought, to know I'd look this good in such an extreme haircut, but I also knew that wasn't the whole point. I looked familiar, but not in a way that I could place.

I stared at myself all the rest of the day, in every mirror and store window I passed, but I couldn't figure it out. Not until I woke up, startled, the next morning at about 4:00. What I looked like, I realized, was a collaborator, one of those sad French girls who'd slept with a Nazi soldier, and after the war the whole village takes its revenge, which includes shaving her head. My god, I thought, was this what he'd intended? A little message about sleeping with the enemy, brought to you—and paid for—by the enemy. I paced around for a few hours with a quilt wrapped around me and a cup of coffee in my hand, distractedly shuttling between my mirror and the window, where a cold gray dawn gathered light.

And then I also had to give Mrs. Branden about a million of my measurements, and she took about a million more, odd sections of my body that I didn't like to think anybody was going to deal with. Which just shows how realistically I was going about this. Of course, if I'd been a more realistic person, no way would I have gotten into this thing in the first place. Then, finally, on a Thursday night just after Halloween, it was showtime.

But it's hard for me to describe those first sweaty, embarrassing couple of weeks. Probably because I looked like such a klutz for so much of it. I like to remember the parts where I felt halfway pretty, and I also like to tell about some of my wisecracks. But those first few agonizing weeks...like, for example, the very first time I actually went to his house after all the fittings and appointments. I was on my knees, trembling with fear and excitement, tethered to a hook in the wall near the fireplace, waiting for him. What would he say, I kept wondering, and what would it really be like to fuck him? I even wondered — I'm embarrassed to admit — if he'd like the haircut. I waited there for about ten minutes, until finally he came in, looked me over impassively, and asked, "How do you greet me?"

Trick question. Of course I didn't know, but I thought of porn novels I'd read, so I put my head down and kissed his shoe. And got my new crimson lipstick, that he'd bought for me to wear, all over the toe. He thwacked me hard with the riding crop he was carrying (I'd never seen a riding crop, but I recognized it from my porn reading) and told me to lick the lipstick off his shoe. And then he said curtly that of course I didn't know how to greet him, because he hadn't told me yet, and that the first thing I should learn was that I shouldn't pretend to know anything I didn't, and to please spare him the benefit of all my damn adolescent jerkoff reading.

28

The thwack from the riding crop was a shock, but it was his cold and contemptuous tone of voice that really got to me, that first time and in the weeks after it. I knew that it was ridiculous to feel this way, but he'd fucking hurt my feelings. Not that he'd been exactly affectionate in our first conversations, but he'd been forthcoming and appreciative. I knew that in the two weeks before I'd begun coming to his house, I'd caught myself replaying bits and snatches of those conversations in my head, and yes, his compliments "you're pretty" and "you're smart"—and even "that beautiful butt"—were among my favorite selections. Pretty soon into the training process, though, I resigned myself to never hearing stuff like that again.

Because that's what it was, training. And even though a big porn reader like me should have known exactly what to expect, I was shocked and insulted. Somehow I'd imagined that of course I'd immediately know how to give him everything he wanted—hell, I thought he'd take care of all that, maybe with mirrors, I don't know. Somehow, when it was me and not O or Jamie or others of my beloved literary bottoms, I'd shifted gears, or genres, in my imagination, thinking it would be more like one of those pseudorape scenes from a novel you buy on a rack in the supermarket—you know, "He held her in his granite-hard grasp, his hungry desire making her swoon." I think I'd expected to do a lot of swooning, while his "hungry desire" did all the work. Wrong.

He did know what he wanted, though—what, when, where, and how. I was amazed, and oddly comforted, that he knew so exactly. I hadn't known that was possible. Nobody I'd ever slept with had known, I thought, considering my last few years of boyfriends. Or if they'd known, they certainly hadn't let me in on it. Even Eric, who had been the major love of my life—we'd played at living together for a few months during my junior year—he hadn't known. We'd been really proud of ourselves, Eric and I—lots of loud sex all the time and everywhere—we'd thought the shower was especially cool. And we'd been considerate, going down on each other as often as we thought the other guy wanted it, though we'd been guessing, really, because we'd both been shy about asking.

Well, forget shy. Jonathan wasn't shy, and he also sure didn't ask. He used precise, grammatical sentences to demand exactly what he wanted, and the operative word was "exactly." And I began to wonder how people ever knew what each other really wanted, without, you know, somebody demanding it. Well, maybe people who'd been married a million years and had hit it by trial and error, but that didn't sound like an attractive way to go about it. So in an odd way I was beginning to think the deal we'd made had a kind of logic and integrity. His getting what he wanted was his right and my obligation was to hit it exactly.

Meanwhile, since most of the time I wasn't even near perfect, he treated me like a new puppy that was constantly making messes. Only he was a whole lot less affectionate than you'd be toward a puppy. Still, if I had to come up with a metaphor for that awkward early period, it would probably be dog obedience school. Not that this would be such an original insight on my part—he set the mood by hanging a humiliating little oval brass tag with the name CARRIE"" etched on it from the new, stiff, brown leather collar Mrs. Branden buckled around my neck those late autumn afternoons.

It was hard, it was humiliating, and worst of all, he hadn't even kept one of his promises—remember that impressive little speech about my being aching, exhausted, and fucked out? A big shocker was that he rarely fucked me, preferring, nine times out of ten, to use my mouth—my mouth and particularly my throat.

And that was embarrassing, because I wasn't even that good at it. I gagged the first few times, defending myself against that moment when he most wanted me defenseless, that moment when not only would my mouth be entirely molded to him and my nose entirely full of his smell, but when my throat would open, when I'd abjure any choice about what went deep, deep down into me.

He was icily patient—"Pay attention," he'd insist—and he beat me a lot, as well. He was abstract, precise, and he scared me; I wondered if it would go on like this forever. I felt I had little choice but to keep trying, and, yeah, I did get better at it, feeling little proofs of my own power in the shuddering strength of his orgasms. Of course he wanted me that way, I realized one late afternoon, looking up at him through a haze of pain and tears. My mouth, that motor-mouth, the orifice that had the most to do with consciousness, intelligence—he wanted me to use it, consciously and intelligently, to learn, adore, accept, and caress his every fold, contour, and smell. And when he was ready to come he wanted to overpower it all, transforming active intelligence into pure receptacle. It was a hell of an exchange, involving a whole lot more than bodily fluids. I became oddly proud to do it.

And then, of course, there was lots of crawling around, ass high, lots of being cuffed, smacked, and thwacked—puppy-like—for clumsiness or messes I'd made (and might have to lick up), lots of strokes of the cane for talking out of turn or disrespectfully. More subtly, maybe, there were the beatings

31

for what, that first time, he'd called "lapses in form or sensibility." This could mean anything at all, I learned, but in practice it usually came down to having gotten too turned on and carried away and not noticing fast enough what he wanted next. Or being overwhelmed by some rare instance of tenderness, like after I fetched him something with my mouth, and he'd taken it and stroked my cheek. And I'd hoped that his hand might come close to my mouth, so I could kiss it, maybe even lick it or suck his finger. And I did, a little, and it was worth it, even though he cuffed me for being sloppy and silly.

Not to worry, though—there really wasn't much tenderness. Just mostly lust. Overriding the awkwardness, incoherence, embarrassment, and confusion there was wall-to-wall, overwhelming, dizzying lust. And even though I'd go home those evenings sore, humiliated, miserable, and vowing never to return, I always did return. Promptly.

And then he switched gears on me. This happened—no kidding—on a dark and stormy night. And if you think I'm trying to make it sound all gothic and sucker you with the pathetic fallacy, well, maybe I am. I mean, it *was* dark and stormy; it was November, after all. And while I don't believe that nature was reflecting my emotional situation, I know that nature was putting me in a mood that matched its wildness. Because I was certainly feeling dark and stormy that night, trudging up the hill with the wind whistling and the rain falling around me, wondering why the hell I was out there just to get my ass whipped.

I can't speak for Jonathan, though, meticulous Jonathan who probably never strayed from his lesson plans, no matter what else was going on. I suspect that any correspondence between his emotional situation and the weather is total coincidence. Or maybe not.

In any case, I was as wet, dark, and stormy as the weather when I rang the kitchen doorbell. Mrs. Branden came to the door, cool, friendly, and quiet, as usual. I took off my clothes, shook off the water, and hung them on a hook in the corner. Then I went to the little room off the kitchen, turned on the very bright light near the little table, and made up my face, very, very carefully, as usual.

I came back into the kitchen and sat down on one of the chairs, and she knelt down to lace up my boots. They were little brown ankle lace-up boots, with hooks at the ankles so I wouldn't need ankle cuffs, and crazily high spool-shaped heels. I could have put them on myself, but the rules were that she was supposed to do it. Then the collar, with its awful name tag, and matching cuffs around my wrists. The collar and cuffs were so stiff that I felt them all the time, even when I wasn't wearing them. She hooked the cuffs together behind my back, attached a leash to the collar, and, as usual, led me down the hall to the study. But this time, instead of leading me to the usual spot near the hook in the wall, she led me to a leather ottoman placed in front of the fire.

"Kneel down on it, put your head down. Get your ass up and spread your legs way apart," she said, in an entirely neutral voice (her deadpan delivery was every bit as good as Jonathan's, probably better). And when I did, she attached the collar's loop to a hook attached to the ottoman, so my face was against the leather. She pushed my knees apart some more and attached the loops at my ankles to two more hooks in the ottoman. Then she put her cool, capable hands at the sides of my hips and angled up my ass a few degrees, lifting it up a little too. And then, silently, she left.

From experience, I knew I'd have to wait for Jonathan. Maybe two minutes, maybe twenty. I always felt fortunate to have this room to wait in—leaded windows, brilliant oriental rug, real art on the walls, books and books and books, though of course I never touched them, and the fire. The room was perhaps a little phony—a little too *Brideshead Revisited* or something. I mean, the rest of the house was airy, simple, some Arts and Crafts and some high tech, more like a house I'd expect him to live in. This study was definitely a stage set, and I liked its hyperreality, its surfeit of deep colors and textures, its thickness, perhaps you could say. Even this evening, with my face pressed against the soft leather, I could still more or less see the fire, hear it crackling. I concentrated on it, partly to drown out the sounds of the wind, the rain, and the evergreens blowing against the windows, not to speak of my thoughts about what was going to happen next. So I missed the sound of Jonathan coming in behind me and started when I felt his hands unhooking my wrists.

"You can use your hands to part your ass some more," he said.

I grabbed the cheeks of my ass and felt a rush of coldness as he pushed some cream all the way up. "Open," he repeated very softly and began, slowly, slowly, to push in a big rubber dildo, the size, I guessed, of his erect cock. He pushed so slowly and so relentlessly and seemed to be tracing such a tortuous, meandering path, that even though I wanted to resist, I couldn't quite find the moment, or the muscular center, for actually doing so. Instead, some part of me was discovering, as he kept breathing the word, that there was a way to be utterly, terrifyingly "open."

He got it all the way in. Perhaps I'd screamed; I was moaning and trembling terribly. I felt coldness again against my ass. There were three little chains attached to the base of the dildo. One went up the crack of my ass toward the base of my spine, while the other two went between my legs, outlining my cunt. All three hung from a little black leather belt that he buckled in back. I recognized the technology—courtesy of Pauline Réage—but the emotions I was feeling were brand-new. It was as though I needed his hands, his voice, his desire. As though, open as I was, I had lost a kind of authority, both against the world and my own gleeful, brute body. I felt as though I would fall into a frightening, devilish space beyond ego and consciousness if I couldn't please and obey him exactly.

He unhooked me and helped me to stand up. And kissed me in a questioning sort of way. Oddly, I found myself kissing him back in a questioning sort of way, too. This was confusing to both of us. His question, I think now, was "What do you feel?" and mine was "What do you want?" but in a deeper way than I'd ever asked before. It was, perhaps, more like "Oh, please, what do you want? I'll die if I can't do what you want." He stepped back and took a moment to consider.

"Does it hurt?" he asked.

"No, Jonathan, it doesn't hurt exactly," I said, searching for words, "but it's different from any feeling I've ever had."

"Well," he said, "let's see what it's all about." He sat down and proceeded to command me to do this and that, all the puppy tricks—walk, stand, sit, squat, beg, crawl, play with myself, fetch things with my mouth. Everything I did seemed oddly amplified. He made me take off all his clothes, and then—the dildo didn't interfere at all—he fucked me for a long, long time on the rug. Afterward, he told me to stand up. He lay under a plaid blanket, up on his elbows, facing me. "Tell me about having this dildo stuffed way up your ass," he said.

I looked down at him. I felt weak, and my pelvis felt bruised and wobbly. I was cold, too, my thighs shivery and slick with sweat and come. I found words, although I was blushing and trembling, and could only speak very slowly. "It makes me feel like a very bad girl, Jonathan," I said hesitantly and very softly.

He spoke very softly too. "But you've been a very good girl tonight, you know. Isn't it odd? Well, don't wear yourself out trying to figure it out." Then he stood up, found his pants on the chair where I'd put them, and pulled off the belt. "Kneel on the armchair and I'll beat you," he said gently, "and then you can turn around and I'll beat you a little on the tits, just until they get pink. Then I'll unplug you and you can sleep here tonight. There's a little bedroom for you upstairs, down the hall from mine. It's too dangerous for you to drive back across the bridge in this storm."

But of course wear myself out trying to figure it out was exactly what I did. Later, my friend Stuart and I would talk endlessly about that night. Stuart and I had been friends since freshman year, but we had become roommates in June, as soon as we graduated. He had continued on as a graduate student in literature, getting the fellowship they probably would have given to me if I'd applied for it. When I limped in, nights I didn't stay over at Jonathan's, he'd rub my shoulders and read to me from François Villon or the Brontës. We shared a big flat in the Mission District with a UPS driver and a magician (well, Jo does office temps for a living and magic at kids' birthday parties, but I think she's good, anyhow). Your typical twenty-something no-future roommate gang, right?—delivery person, office worker/magician, grad student, bike messenger/sex slave—your low-wage, nonproductive, postindustrial workforce in miniature.

Only Stuart knew about my life with Jonathan, though Jo and Henry were sweet and wouldn't have cared. Still, I didn't want anybody but Stuart to know—it was too difficult to explain, too difficult even for me to understand.

Stuart was, as he put it, more or less bi, but mostly shy. So, though I did certainly listen to his stories about his love life, and pet and comfort him when he needed it, the unfair truth was that he really couldn't compete with this amazing continuing story I had going and my endless need for comfort. Add to that this other thing we had become addicted to at school, theory. Lying across Stuart's big bed and talking ourselves silly trying to understand the Jonathan story was how we lived. Was there any other way?

"So maybe it's all just, like, object relations?" I'd muse. "*Civilization and Its Discontents?* Fuckin' boring early socialization? Or how about we make it more politically correct object relations—Jonathan was never nurtured by his rich father."

Stuart considered. "Well, I think we want an object relations theory that's at least got a little more philosophical oomph to it. I'd add in all that Hegelian master/slave stuff. Self knowing itself by dominating the other, but not devouring the other completely because that blows the game. Some of that seems true enough, anyhow, though you look in no danger of being devoured completely, at least when you wear your messenger clothes.

"All that basic social science stuff we had to sit through seems true enough, if you want to explain what's going on as a pathology. Which I don't. Not when it gives you such great sex and me such great voyeuristic entertainment. You're my heroine." And he stopped being helpful and supportive and just looked expectant.

"Okay, yes, okay," I sighed, as I often did. "Yes, you can see the new welts. You can touch them very lightly. First bring me a cup of cocoa with rum in it and two marshmallows. And turn the TV to *Cheers*."

CHAPTER II

Krazy Kat

I didn't exactly believe any of the theories, but it did look like Jonathan and I had found, as it were, a groove. When, soon afterward, he started fucking me up the ass regularly, I found myself thanking him, which wasn't according to the rules he'd laid down, but became an extension of them, my own little improvisation, I guess. As a graduation present, he replaced the hated puppy collar and boots with sleek black leather. That isn't to say that there weren't still whacks, beatings, and humiliations. That was, after all, the game we were playing. But one thing I did know, perhaps the one generality all the theory was good for, was that the game was played at some precarious balance point, teetering on the edge of shame and the shadow boundary of civilization. That we played this game mostly in that hypercivilized study, among all the art, books, and old furniture, was, I was sure, an ironic signifier he meant us to share. I appreciated that, whenever I was in any condition to appreciate things like that.

As the winter wore on, he brought more toys—angry little clips for the nipples and other soft parts, sometimes with little bells attached. He told Mrs. Branden to give me a cup of coffee when I came in and not to let me pee; this would increase the chances that I'd have to squat over the chamber pot he kept for me in the corner. And if I dribbled onto the floor, I'd have to lick up the drops.

He tried different whips on me—whips and broad leather paddles. Once "just for the hell of it," he said, he tried a stiff hairbrush, which really hurt. Another time, an old-fashioned shaving strop—he'd ordered it from a catalog, Peterman or something, just to use it on me; I don't think he ever used it to shave with. There was a period—Christmas and through January—when he seemed to have presents for me all the time. Things that hurt and humiliated, which sometimes I'd find beautifully wrapped under a little holiday tree in his study and have to unwrap—of course without tearing the paper—and thank him for. Sometimes I would never have seen them before—strange Victorian posture-training devices, for example—and he'd make me guess what I thought they were for before he showed me.

And then, after the needles of the little Christmas tree dried up and it got tossed into the alley, there were costumes. Not every time—lots of times he still wanted me naked except for the collar and cuffs—but sometimes, not when I could predict, when I came to the kitchen door there'd be costumes for me to wear. Tight, tight little corsets around my waist with elaborate garter arrangements hanging off them. Black, mostly, but sometimes antique white muslin or canvas, for all I knew with real whalebone. The corsets' laces and hooks drove composed Mrs. Branden to distraction. She'd actually have to prop her knee against my ass, like in an eighteenth-century engraving, to be able to pull hard enough on the laces. She'd sweat and curse, too, and once she slapped me afterward in frustration.

If the corsets were period pieces, though, the shoes provided an eclectic counterpoint, as well as an endless outlet for what, evidently, was Jonathan's trashy side—just in case, like me, you hadn't thought he had one. Well, it was shoes— glitzy, extreme torments for the ankle and instep. Where did he get them, I'd wonder, the six- inch spikes in silver lamé, or purple glitter, or backless with a million little straps? Where drag queens got theirs, I supposed, or Tina Turner. To wear with them, there were seamed black stockings, which he liked to see in shreds by the end of an evening.

I'd sometimes think, as Mrs. Branden was tricking me out in this stuff, about what he'd said that first afternoon, about my being willing to put up with the trite details. It was true. I was, and so was he. Well, actually, he was a whole lot more than willing to put up with it—he was utterly, sincerely delighted with Barbie Doll stuff that you'd think he'd be too sophisticated for. The first time, for example, that I wore the white, antique, maybe-whalebone corset, he walked slowly around me. "Oh, yes," he said dreamily.

I hadn't realized originally, even with all my reading and fantasizing, exactly how these fetishistic props worked. It was only after a couple of times wearing them that I'd really gotten it—the way the different elements, these technologies of the profane, worked in ensemble. I began to see and feel now how the corset, when worn with the ridiculously high heels, would thrust my ass out. How my breasts would be pushed forward, while the high collar forced me to keep my back straight and my head up. Sometimes I felt as though my body wasn't mine at all, but his, forced into a configuration to make it maximally accessible to him, giving me no place to hide. And sometimes I'd be embarrassed to realize that I wanted to hold my body that way in front of him—that I was grateful for the para- phernalia that gave me no choice but to display myself so outrageously. And mostly, I guess, it was a battle inside me between both of those attitudes, neither of which I could entirely control, both of which kept me off balance.

That afternoon, anyhow, his "oh yes" made me almost dizzy with a kind of power. I loved the feeling of getting him that hot. He pressed against my front, put his hands on my ass, and kissed my shoulders. "Do you think," he murmured, "that Emily Dickinson wore one of these corsets? Under those white dresses, you know."

A question I hadn't expected. Well, he had promised he'd stay ahead of me, hadn't he? I tried to keep a straight, respectful face. "I don't know, Jonathan. I don't really think so, but I don't know."

"It would have been the right historical period, wouldn't it?" he said, rubbing and pinching the bottom of my ass. "And if Emily didn't, what about that sister-in-law? The one who fucked on the pool table."

Southern belles wore them, I thought. And he was right, they were Emily's contemporaries. But I knew he wouldn't be interested in plantation ladies in big hoop skirts saying, "Fiddle-de-dee, Rhett." His thing would be to wonder about a spooky woman who could write a line like "I like a look of agony/because I know it's true." Still, were the corsets also worn up north in abolitionist Amherst, Mass.? I had to insist on my ignorance, about both Emily and Susan, the randy sister-in-law, while Jonathan maneuvered us toward the couch. "And I thought you were so well educated," he said. "Good thing I'm educating you now."

He sat down on the couch, forcing me to my knees in front of him, and kissed me, holding my breasts in his hands. He often did this, playing with my nipples, making them as

42

hard as cherry stones. It was usually a prelude to his putting clips on them, but even though I knew this, my nipples would always stiffen obediently, humiliatingly to his touch. *I* might have my streaks of waywardness; *they* never seemed to. This time, though, he didn't stop. He kept kissing me, probing my mouth with his tongue while he rolled my nipples between his fingers. I gave up trying to figure out what he wanted; as far as I could see, he wanted to be doing this. I should have been alarmed—what was I missing? what was he going to punish me for?—but I felt too wonderful, too warm and loose, and a beating seemed like a small price to pay.

He loosened my collar. It was still plenty tight, but his moving the buckles one hole over (or so it felt), allowed me just a little more movement, a little more ability to throw my head back, to gasp, shudder, and moan.

He moved his mouth to one of my breasts, and one of his hands to my cunt. His tongue and fingers were insistent, probing, and patient. He had great hands. Once in a while he'd make one of those impossibly delicate model buildings that architects, amazingly, still make in this electronically mediated day and age. I mean, I never saw him at work, but it would be there in the study, glue and X-acto knife on the shelf, growing in size and complexity for a week or so, and I'd go weak with lust, imagining his long fingers cutting and pasting the tiny strips of balsa wood and foam core.

Right now one—no, two—of those fingers were slowly moving up my asshole, while one from the other hand continued to make tiny circles on my clit. It felt like he'd go on forever, or as long as it would take me to feel as absolutely spectacular as I could possibly feel. I felt like a puppet, as though there were strings attached to my breast and cunt, and they were being tugged, ever so lightly, insistently, making me swoop and dance. I gave in, finally, howling and even laughing a little, hoarsely, deep in my throat, and collapsed against him, trying to catch my breath but dimly aware of the volcanic sensations that were still there inside me.

"Lie down on the floor," he whispered into my neck, and began to push me down by the shoulders. I followed the pressure of his hands and found myself on my back. He knelt beside me, pushed my knees up, so that my legs were bent, parted them, and started nibbling slowly at the insides of my thighs, right above the black stockings. I could feel him licking, chewing a little, kissing — lips, teeth, and tongue all somehow getting into the act as though my flesh were some kind of complex salad that he was savoring thoughtfully.

I felt my belly quivering under the tightly laced corset. And yes, his mouth was moving upward, slowly, almost absentmindedly, but definitely toward my cunt, parting it with his tongue, while his hands on my hipbones held me still. I wanted to move more, to buck. The quiver in my belly spread and rippled, centrifugally. Part of me wanted to try to throw him off — I was almost afraid of the sensations, the intensity of not just his tongue, but his breath as well. It was his warm, even breathing that I could feel up my cunt, that seemed so invasive, in its tiny way, and that was making me moan — was I moaning? I guessed so. But he wouldn't let me throw him off, I knew, and realized that truly, I didn't want him ever to stop. All I could do was rock my pelvis back and forth, meeting his tongue, chasing it, and then retreating, pretending to hide from it, and finally just surrendering to it, moaning and then yelling until everything exploded and first I was falling from a very great height and then I was a puddle on the rug, the winter afternoon light slanting in on me through the leaded windows.

He sat next to me for I don't know how long, tracing the intricate stitchery of the corset with his finger. Then, finally, he got back up on the couch and said, "Kneel up straight." Now, I thought, wincing, I'll find out what I didn't do—what it was he had really wanted. I looked up at him, lounging with his arms spread against the top of the couch and his legs crossed. And I wondered what I should be doing right now. Should I be thanking him, worshiping him in some way I should know but didn't? Should I be doing anything at all except feeling splendidly drained and exhausted? He didn't look angry or even stern, though he did look thoughtful.

"Well," he said, looking at me carefully.

I didn't know what to say, just stared at him through a kind of haze, as he reached down and tightened the buckles on my collar. "Well, okay," he said, smiling. "I like the way you look right now. You look surprised and grateful, and frightened and confused, too. Perfect.

"That," he continued, "was as nice as beating you or coming in your ass. Different, of course, but lovely all the same. I've wanted to do it for a while, you know, but it wouldn't have worked out. But I can tell you that I haven't enjoyed holding back on it all these months."

I had only a faint understanding of what he was getting at. Actually, at that moment, it took just about everything I had to keep myself upright and scraped off the floor. He wasn't going to punish me, I was dimly realizing. That was good, anyway. He was telling me something that he thought was important, and I knew I had to listen, though all I wanted to do at that moment was live happily ever after in the way my body was feeling. And to sleep, upstairs in his bed with the window open and a breeze drifting in...

"Listen to me," he said, raising my chin and slapping my cheek lightly.

"Yes, Jonathan," I murmured. "I'm sorry, Jonathan."

"That's better," he said. "God," he continued, "I love to see you following the rules when you really don't want to. Well, but that's why we have rules, isn't it?"

I murmured my assent, according to the rules. Right, the goddamn rules, and I could feel the world he'd built around us taking shape again, disrupting my idyll. This catechism was going to take some time, I was beginning to realize, and I was also beginning to realize that I wasn't going to enjoy it very much.

"And you've learned a lot, haven't you?" He was deep into pedantic mode now. "I mean, you're still far from perfect, but you'll continue to improve. You've learned to be open and available and attentive to me. You've learned to accept punishment from me. Well, punishment isn't so difficult, I guess, compared to gratuitous whimsical pain—pain that I've created simply because I feel like it. If I want to see marks on your thighs, I put them there, right? If I want to see you in tears, I make that happen. And now you're learning that if I want to make you entirely delighted, I can do that, too."

I had, believe it or not, forgotten that that's supposed to be the point of a sexual relationship—usually, that is. Which was more or less what he was saying, now. "The night you met me, at that stupid party, you imagined my taking you home and making you feel this way, didn't you?"

"Yes, Jonathan, I did," I admitted softly. This was about as humiliating as anything I'd been through with him.

"Well, why shouldn't you have?" he said. "You deserve it. Someday maybe you'll find somebody just as attractive and deserving as you are and the two of you will burn up the sheets every night, while you get your PhDs and write books and have babies, all that good stuff.

"Only," he continued, "that's not what I want, and it seems that it's not what you want either, at least for now. So we're doing...well, you know what we're doing. I've held back all these months on making love to you this way because you would have misunderstood if I had done it any earlier. And I'm still not sure you understand completely. I didn't want you to expect to feel like this, or even to think of it as a treat or a reward. Don't expect it. Don't anticipate it. I'll do it when I feel like doing it, and you won't be able to predict it. And don't try any tricks to make me feel like doing it. I'll punish you very severely if I ever think that's what you're up to. Got that?"

"Yes, Jonathan," I murmured, quite miserably.

"Yes, I think you do," he said, and then unceremoniously unzipped his pants. "Well," he continued, "my turn now. Open your mouth."

And afterward, he simply sent me home, telling me that was enough for today. As I was getting dressed I remembered an old musical, *Carousel,* that they'd done at my high school. Songs like "My Boy Bill" and "You'll Never Walk Alone." We all sneered at its corniness, but secretly I'd loved it: I'd cry at the thought of never, never knowing that someone loved me.

And I'd fall asleep trying to imagine a slap that felt like a kiss. I still couldn't quite imagine such a slap. But trust Jonathan to teach me about kisses that felt like slaps.

And that was the end of my apprenticeship. That was, in a sense, the golden lesson at the end of the rainbow. No matter what happened between us it was all consequence and actualization of his utter monopoly of power. He'd proved it to me that winter afternoon, like the bomb at Alamogordo had proved Einstein's physics. Not that I would have denied it before, but now I knew, consciously knew, that there was no second-guessing him. It was a relief in some ways, a letting go. I simply relaxed into it, as though I were beginning to dream in a foreign language—a language of beatings and humiliations, of rare, extravagant pleasure, rituals, formalities. It was a complicated and mysteriously involving language, for all that it was based on only one deep syntactical structure, one rule once again, the rule of his saying, "I want."

And—I'll confess it to you here—I loved to hear him say, "I want." I'd meditate on it. I'd hear it like a mantra. I got off on thinking how privileged he was. Once, during my last weeks of school, I had to go to the women's room of the library to jerk off, just from thinking about how exquisitely, consistently unfair it all was. Well, I'd also been reading some theory that seemed quite apposite to my situation. It seemed as though everything we were assigned that semester was about sex—every text in the canon was really an eroticized, sadomasochistic version of some other text. Intellectually, I didn't quite approve: there must be more to life than sex and power, I'd think, even if there wasn't much more to my life at that time. But given my inability to concentrate on anything else, I figured I'd lucked out. In a sense, you could say that it was Jonathan who got me through my last semester.

On the surface, my life at school didn't change at all. I wrote my papers, I hung out with friends, some of whom knew I had some mysterious relationship with a guy in the city and accepted the fact that I wasn't going to tell them any more than that. About the only day-to-day thing about my life that changed was that I ran instead of swimming for exercise that spring—well, I couldn't change in the locker room anymore, could I?

In March, I got a thrilling letter saying that one of my papers was going to be published in an obscure academic journal—I'd submitted it the previous fall. The professor who'd persuaded me to submit it insisted on opening a bottle of champagne that he kept in a little refrigerator in his office—for first publications, he said. I just kept reading the letter, over and over again, until I had it memorized.

That was the only time I ever got to Jonathan's late, fifteen whole minutes. And buzzed on champagne, too—lucky I didn't get killed driving over on the bridge. I remember Jonathan's look of dark concern and restrained anger when Mrs. Branden led me in, flushed and spacey. He asked me why I was late, and I remember the transformation his expression took—God, he has a warm, lovely smile, I thought—when I told him about the publication.

"That's terrific, really terrific, Carrie," he said, taking the chain off my collar. "God, that's really great, I knew you could do it. Now go get the cane so I can give you five for being late."

So my life continued, weird and schizy, but with a kind of logic. It was the future that I couldn't deal with. I mean I had no problem leading this double life while I was an undergraduate, but I couldn't make myself fill out graduate school applications. Later for graduate school, I kept thinking. Later for any future at all. I felt as though I was in the middle of reading—of living—this epic story, and it was all I could do to keep turning the pages fast enough. Everything else would have to wait.

Application deadlines passed and I didn't care. I started telling people that I was going to take a year off. I even had an elaborate song and dance worked out about how you couldn't really know postmodern America until you'd put in some time as a slacker. I said this a lot, I think, until one day I goofed and said "slave" instead of "slacker." People thought I meant wage slave, so it was okay, but I never said it again.

I wondered, now and again, if I weren't becoming some kind of crazed cultist, a Manson girl, a Moonie. Was I throwing my promising life away? But I didn't think so. I mean, I would have done—come on, I *did*—everything Jonathan told me to do, but it was a different kind of doing what I was told than selling flowers in airports. And I didn't think it was my whole life. It was just what was happening to me exactly then, in the present tense. Anyhow, as soon as I graduated, I got my bike messenger job. Jonathan had never asked me my plans. I guess he'd been confident, in that smug way of his, that I'd be around for a while. Definitely not flattering, but I was beyond finding any of this flattering. I just wanted it to continue, to develop, to take its mysterious course. I thought of us like Krazy Kat and Ignatz, or Wile E. Coyote and the Road Runner, an eternal couple, enacting the endless themes and variations of power and desire, ingenuity and redundancy and pain. Someday, I thought, I would look down and see that I was standing on thin air, and then I'd go plummeting to earth. But that was someday, not now. I was glad that when I announced that my schedule was changing, he added a few more hours a week to our routine.

In July, a month or so after I'd graduated, Jonathan told me that he had to go to Chicago for two weeks on a business project.

"I want you to come with me," he said. "It would be bad to break our momentum, and anyhow, I don't want to go that long without doing this."

Obediently—I was on my knees in front of him, back arched—I said I'd find out if I could take some time off work. Actually, the idea sounded pretty awful to me. Chicago in August. Probably he'd allow me to wander around the Art Institute a couple of hours a day while he was working and the maid cleaned the hotel room. Then I'd probably have to wait on my knees for god knew how long until he got back from work, all tense and stressed with yuppie workaholism, tie loosened, oxford cloth shirt and suspenders all sweaty from muggy Chicago. Perhaps, I thought, he'd hire somebody to come in and chain me up an hour or so before he was going to get back (though he'd always get back at least an hour later than he'd planned).

Concretely, the idea sucked, I thought. Abstractly, though, I discovered that I found it somewhat exciting. I was turned on by the purely objective, instrumental quality of my situation. Why shouldn't he bring his slave along, I thought. Why have a slave unless you could have her there to stick yourself into when you were hot, stressed, and exhausted? I thought I could arrange the time off. That was one of the good parts of being a bike messenger. I promised to try.

He stroked my breasts and shoulders and kissed my forehead softly. "Undress me," he whispered, and I started with his shoes, as he'd taught me, unlacing them with my teeth. He helped me, taking off his shirt, unzipping his pants. We were both very turned on; I realized that we were both imagining this trip, though I'll never know if our fantasy images matched or not. Everything was going very slowly, as though we were already moving sweatily through heavy, moist air (though in fact it was fifty degrees outside — gray San Francisco summer weather). I sucked him, rolling his balls around my mouth while he stroked my face.

Then he pulled away from me and told me to choose a whip from the cabinet where they were hanging on hooks. He had several, of different styles. As though in a dream, I chose the heavier of the two cat-o'-nine-tails. It had knotted ends. Why did I pick the heavier one? Maybe I wanted to be hurt more, or I knew he liked that one more, or (this is the way I really remember it) I simply thought it was a prettier whip. I handed it to him silently, and he flicked it lightly over my breasts. "You don't have to count," he said. I nodded. I knew he meant that he wouldn't need the sound of my voice to tell him when I'd had as much as I could take. That he'd know.

He chained my hands above me and whipped me, almost languorously, from my knees to my shoulders, front and back, the whole strike zone. It felt like millions of little stings, again and again and again and again. I gasped and groaned, and tried to keep my eyes on him, his thighs, the muscles in his forearms, his mouth, his beautiful, erect, reddened cock, with the veins so elegantly articulated and clearly standing out. When he unchained me I slumped against him, and he picked me up. I wrapped my legs around his waist, hungrily and

52

impatiently trying to angle toward his cock, which I didn't think I could bear not having in me another moment. I knew I wasn't supposed to act so aggressively, but I didn't care. What was he going to do, beat me some more? I knew he didn't want to. I knew that he wanted to be inside. He sat us down in his armchair, moving me up and down, his hands on my burning ass, his mouth on my neck, my breasts. I felt teeth, I think.

And then later, after we'd both come, there was still his mouth, all over my face, my neck, and me kissing him back, just as hungrily and furiously, the both of us banging teeth against jawbones as though we both wanted to eat the other alive, as though all the whipping and fucking had not been enough, and we didn't know what would be. I stayed on his lap for quite a while until we got our breaths back, and then I slid off and he got up and we did eat each other, first him, then me, until we both had enough energy to fuck again, this time, though, in his bed—"We should get to do this comfortably once in a while, damn it," he said, leading me up the stairs—and then to nap a little, until he unbuckled my collar and sent me away, first to raid the refrigerator and then to fall into a deep sleep in my bed in the little room down the hall.

But I never made it to Chicago. I drifted to work the next morning, feeling like Scarlett O'Hara after the big staircase scene. I liked playing the lurid moments over in my head, and I found myself giggling when I remembered him insisting on fucking in his bed that second time. It was, I guessed, our own little staircase scene.

And then I got to work and forgot about everything. Because things were wildly disorganized. One of their most dependable messengers had gotten injured the day before, and somebody else had quit. So I really had to hustle all day, and when I finally got a chance to ask for the time off, they told me they were too short-staffed and I was too new. I was disappointed and a little scared of what Jonathan would say. I was right to be scared, too. He didn't say much when I told him I couldn't come, but his eyes got stormy and his jaw twitched. And all the sweaty honeymoon vibes in the room iced over. "It's not your fault," was all he said, which sounded a lot to me like, "I wish it were your fault so that I could cane you within an inch of your life."

He found reasons to cane me anyway, of course. I mean, it wasn't that hard, since he was making up the rules. Things got very formal, very difficult, almost like the early times I'd spent with him.

This time, though, it wasn't my inexperience that was causing the problems. It was our arrangement itself: the emotional challenge of shuttling between real life and whatever it was we were doing in Jonathan's study. I took this seriously. I think Jonathan hoped I'd volunteer to quit my messenger job, but I wasn't about to do that, and he wasn't about to ask me to. So things were not exactly fun for the next week, until Jonathan left for Chicago. I kept coming to his house, kept getting criticized and beaten, spent a lot of time with painful clips on my nipples, didn't get fucked at all except stiffly, painfully, up the ass. And, yes, I accepted it all without second-guessing it. He would do it some other way, I thought stoically, when he felt like it.

What I wasn't prepared for was my almost instant horniness after he'd left. I'd planned, of course, to get lots of rest, read a couple of the books I'd pretended to have already read, that sort of thing. But I found myself nodding off over books and waking up with my hand up my cunt. Okay, I thought, that's just how it is, he'll be back soon enough. But I was no longer "aching, exhausted, and fucked out," and I missed it. And, well, I started to look around me.

And found Kevin. Actually, I suppose it's more accurate to say that he found me. I mean, I'd been half noticing him for a few weeks. And if I'd stopped to think about it—which I hadn't, quite—I would have become aware that he'd been making himself very noticeable, lounging around the lobby of one of the buildings I delivered to a lot, a rather glamorous retrofitted brick coffee factory that now housed computer programmers. He was doing something to the air-condition-ing system, something with the ducts—he told me what, but I don't really remember much except that it paid well and he was a member of the Boilermakers' Union. Well, for a few weeks now there he'd been, always in the corner of my eye in that beautiful retro marble lobby. He wore torn overalls, wonderful artful rips and holes in them with bright ski under-wear underneath. He had blue eyes and pink cheeks in a beautiful boy's face under a backward baseball cap, with ten-drils of dirty blond hair peeking out. I noticed his shoes, too, for some reason, dusty L'il Abner work shoes that looked like they had iron in their toes. Maybe Jonathan was turning me into a shoe freak.

When you retrace certain paths fairly regularly during your workday there are some people you semiconsciously depend on seeing and smiling at, receptionists or homeless people or flower vendors. Kevin had become part of the tex-ture of my workweek, one of the prettiest parts, I've got to say, but still just part of the background scenery. I mean, Jonathan pretty much hogged the foreground.

But all of a sudden Jonathan was gone and I was horny and opening my eyes, it seemed, to the world around me. God, I thought, one day in the middle of the first week, doesn't that cute guy with the baseball cap ever do any work around here? How come he's always hanging around when I come through? Oh. Brilliant, Carrie, I thought next. Well then. "Hi," I said. Brilliant again.

Brilliant didn't seem to be necessary, though. He rode up the elevator with me, asking my name and telling me his, while I realized just how pretty he was and how astonishing it was that I'd paid him so little attention these weeks. I'd always been turned on by boys like him—they made me feel simple, goofy, and sexually voracious. I was a little disappointed that he didn't turn off the elevator in midascent—don't all those construction guys know how to do that, with those big bunches of keys that they carry around? But he didn't, or didn't want to. He just acted simple and goofy, too, on that elevator ride and all the ones to follow. By Friday, he'd asked me to have dinner at his house.

"This is a really terrible idea," Stuart insisted that Friday night. "It's a great dress, but we should go dancing or something. This dinner thing is not going to work."

It was a great dress, droopy flowered silk that buttoned down the front. A genuine thrift store find that looked wonderful with socks and combat boots. And I was having a wonderful time getting dressed up for a date.

"Damn it," I said. "Why can't I be doing this? Jonathan didn't say I couldn't fuck anybody else; he just said I wouldn't. And anyhow, maybe I won't."

"Right," he said. "Carrie, you've been panting and slobbering over this guy all week. You are going to hop into bed with him and you are going to be very sorry. Just how dumb are you being here? I mean, don't you think he's going to notice that you've got welts on your ass?"

"I'll think of something," I said.

And I did.

Dinner was fine—he'd pulled it together from a designer pasta store—and we'd just barely been able to keep a conversation going. His job. My job. Ducts. But there was great eye contact and lots of accidental touching when we reached for the bread or wine. It was sweet, embarrassing, horny, suffused with a sense that something was going to happen. He lived far out in the avenues, a block or two from Ocean Beach, on one of those great plain little streets that smell like the ocean and look perpetually scrubbed by the thick fog. We went for a walk on the beach after dinner, froze our asses off, and ran giggling back to his flat, pulling off all the layers of his sweaters that we'd piled on. He was just about to reach for my hand, I think, but I had bigger plans, if only I could get the timing just right. Okay, Carrie, I thought, one…two…hit it.

"Take off all your clothes, Kevin," I said calmly, though it came out about an octave higher than I usually spoke. He was so shocked that it gave me a minute to catch my breath and repitch my voice. I settled down on his couch, crossing my legs and calmly unbuttoning the last sweater.

"You heard me," I continued (much better). "I want to look at you. All of you."

I thought, for a wild instant, that he might strangle me. Scenes from *Looking for Mr. Goodbar* flashed across my line of sight. But no. He stood there frozen for a long moment, and I watched his eyes widen and glaze and his mouth hang open. I recognized the look; sometimes Jonathan liked to make me look in a mirror while he buggered me. And then, slowly, he began to unbutton his shirt.

"Come on," I said, with just a touch of impatience. And yes, he hurried up a bit. I felt a rush—wow, there's nothing quite like power. I can do this, I thought. Waddya know?

But he was taking too long unbuckling his belt. Perhaps his hands were trembling or sweaty. How do you move this along? I wondered.

"You're very clumsy," I observed. "Come here. Put your hands down for a minute." I took off his old black Garrison belt and played around with it. I doubled it, slapping my palm lightly. He looked at it in my hands, and quickly and rather fearfully took off the rest of his clothes.

"Shoes and socks, too," I said. And there he was—blond and blue-eyed and pink-cheeked with a small sweet round butt, golden hair dusting his big arms, and one of those monstrous boyish vertical erections. I looked at it hungrily and he looked at me as though he wanted to die.

"It's not that bad, is it?" I asked. (Jeez, you couldn't relax for a second, could you? I mean, you had to keep the scene moving along. I'd never realized.) He shook his head, mutely.

"My name," I said, "is Carrie. You know that. You can talk to me if you want. I'm going to call you, uh...Lucky."

He didn't seem to get it, and I wondered why I'd thrown in that gratuitous bit of snobby cruelty. Some day, I thought, a wife or girlfriend would drag him to a performance of *Waiting for Godot* and his whole evening, his whole week, would be ruined. Probably I was cruel because I was so nervous, so scared of making a botch of this.

"Kneel down in front of me, Lucky," I said. When he had, I looped his belt around his neck like a leash. I held his back hair in my other hand and angled his head upward so I could kiss him. He tasted sweet. Partly it was the wine we'd had and partly it was him.

I unlooped the belt from around his neck, but I held his head still, staring at him. He looked hypnotized.

"Unbutton my dress," I said. The dress had two dozen little antique pewter buttons running down the front. He reached for the top buttons and I smacked him on the ass with the belt.

"With your teeth," I said.

It's not easy, you know, unbuttoning buttons with your teeth. But Kevin did remarkably well, getting down to my waist, while I stroked his hair and gave his ass teeny little slaps. And then I thought he might really beat me up in complete frustration, so I quickly undid a few more of them myself.

"Take off my underpants," I continued. "And I'll let you use your hands for that. But thank me, first."

Talking's the hardest part, I think. It brings your mind, your consciousness, into play, makes you admit to yourself that it's you who's bearing all this humiliation, not just your dumb animal body. Kevin gave me a look of pure misery, opened and closed his mouth a few times, and finally muttered "thank you," so unhappily that I didn't have the heart to make him add "Carrie."

He pulled off my underpants quickly, and I pushed his face into my cunt. He started licking and nibbling and was doing just wonderfully, I thought. I started to relax, to rest up from all the stage managing I'd been doing. Oh, yum yum yum, I thought, this is more like it. But no it wasn't, it seems, because he evidently felt really ripped off by this — or, more likely, my asking him to talk had simply humiliated him past his limit and he wanted a reward, now.

So he raised his head and scowled at me in a menacing way. And I suddenly realized that he really was a very strong boy and that I didn't think I wanted to keep pushing my luck. And also, or perhaps mostly, I've got to admit that it was hard work keeping this thing going and my invention had just about run out.

"Okay, Kevin," I said agreeably, "something for you now," and slid down between his legs. I gulped down his cock, which was, if anything, standing up even straighter than before. I don't think I could have dealt with it all if Jonathan hadn't been such a stickler for getting deep into my throat. And I don't actually think Kevin meant to come in my mouth — I don't think he was the kind of boy who did that on a first date. But he hadn't had a date like this before, and he was really out of control; he came and came and came, messily, his come drooling down my chin. All in all, though, I thought that he deserved it, and I was actually quite happy to oblige.

He was pretty exhausted afterward and took advantage of that to roll over on his side and avoid looking at me for a while. Finally, I inched over to him and stroked his head shyly.

"Do you hate me, Kevin?" I asked.

He turned around and I could see that he was mainly okay. I mean, he had just come enormously, and that must have helped some. He traced the white crust of dried come on my chin with his finger and looked ridiculously proud of himself. "Nah," he said, "but you are definitely weird, Carrie. Do you, like, do that all the time? March around in rubber outfits, too?"

What to tell? He deserved the truth, I thought. So I told him, well, a version of the truth—sort of the *Reader's' Digest* Condensed Version, anyway. I was like, "Uh, well, there's this guy Jonathan, and I go over to his house sometimes…," telling him the story of me and Jonathan, Lite, which I thought was quite enough. But I did show him the welts on my ass, and they put him pretty much in awe.

And then he got this really strange expression on his face. Finally he took a deep breath and said, "Well, what the fuck, I have something to sort of confess to you." He got up and was gone for a few minutes, and when he came back he was holding a pair of handcuffs.

"I had these in my bedroom," he said, "in the drawer of my bed table. I copped them from an uncle about a year ago. He's been retired from the force for a while, and I saw them in his desk drawer, and I…oh, you know, I mean on TV, "LA Law" and like that, people are always using handcuffs. It was sort of my image of really sophisticated sex, and I thought that maybe I'd have the guts to try it with you. I mean, I've been hot all week, thinking of you cuffed to my bed. I don't know if I'd've really done it, though."

Well, I had to admit he'd gotten certain things right. At least in general, though his specifics were way off. Handcuffs— the one element from that whole *Mr. Benson*/Folsom Street faggot phantasmagoria that has leaked into the mainstream cultural imagery of fancy sex—have just never seemed sexy to me. Maybe I never thought the policeman was my friend, or my enemy either, when I was a kid, and maybe lots of people did. Whatever, for me it will always be collars, corsets, riding crops, and spike heels. But Kevin obviously thought handcuffs were where it was at, and who was I to criticize? "They must really hurt your wrists," I said, politely, running my finger around the inside.

"Oh, they do," he said eagerly, and then he blushed a little. I guess he'd tried them on. I kissed him on the neck and snuggled against him, and pretty soon we were, well, I guess you'd have to say we were making out. And, yeah, he got his wish. He triumphantly carried me to his bedroom and cuffed me to his headboard, and I'm here to tell you that they do hurt your wrists. But he was as happy as could be and politely used a condom, which was good because the truth is that I might not have insisted on it, not really having thought this thing out very well at all. In any case, I certainly liked having him inside me, even with the silly handcuffs. And I owed him one for Lucky, I thought, and I also thought that I owed him because he'd helped me to find out something about myself. Even if it was something as silly and obvious as the fact that I am one complete washout as a top.

Well, my klutzy adventure with Kevin at least relieved some of the horniness, and I actually did get some reading done before Jonathan came back. I enjoyed the rest of my little vacation, but I was eager for his return. Trying out his role, and being so inept at it, made me appreciate him in a way that I hadn't before. I remembered the night we'd met, when he'd told me he thought I'd be good at S/M. I remembered him calmly assuring me that he was good at it. He was, I realized. He really was. I couldn't wait for him to get back so we could play hardball again.

The Saturday he returned, Mrs. Branden laced me into a corset, this time a black one, pulling the laces unbelievably tightly. When he came in, he unhooked the leash from my collar. "Stand up," he said. "Let me look at you."

I stood very still, and so did he, while he stared. He looked pale, tired, drained. And beautiful, as always. More beautiful, but then I always thought that about him when he was stressed in some way. Finally, wordlessly, he put his finger through the ring in my collar and, with his other hand, slapped my face hard. Then he stepped back and crossed his arms. He didn't seem as angry as the slap would have indicated. He seemed a little spooky.

"It was most probably a boy," he said thoughtfully. "A girl would have been more interesting to me, but it was a boy, wasn't it? So what kind of a boy, Carrie? Another messenger, or some punky poet type? Or perhaps both of those things? Maybe a pierced nose or something. Well?"

How the fuck did he know? I mean, I didn't show marks or anything. Hell, I was still showing *his* marks. But I looked different, I guess. Probably, ironically, it was the kind of appreciation I was feeling, my pleasure in just how good he was at taking control. Probably he was noticing that appreciative appraisal, and the brand-new little bit of canniness, of emotional detachment, that made it possible. He must have recognized that some balance had shifted, that he was no longer my whole sexual world. It was a subtle difference, but those are the ones that count, aren't they? And those are the ones that you always let show if you're as bad a liar and keeper of secrets as I am.

"I have a friend," he continued. "She's a genius at discipline. She's got three slaves who adore her. And she plays poker with them. They're naked on silk pillows and she punishes them very severely if they—or their bodies—give away any information about which cards they're holding. It's quite exquisite. Maybe I'll take you there some time. She'd flay you alive."

He slapped me again. "You haven't answered my question. Boy or girl?"

He'd been right about us losing momentum. Two weeks away from him made all of this seem odder than it might have before he'd gone. Did his rights over me really extend to reading my mind? Now that he was back, I wasn't sure. And anyhow, I thought, if he hadn't wanted me to fuck anybody else he should have said so, instead of relying on that original macho little speech about how I wouldn't want to. Kevin and I'd used a condom, I assured myself self-righteously—forgetting that we might not have if it had been up to me—so what was the big deal? Sometimes he really could be tedious.

"It *could* have been a man or a woman or a boy or a girl, Jonathan," I said, slowly and distinctly. "It was a boy."

He took a deep breath, turned around, and stared out the window for a minute. When he turned back again to look at me, his face was composed back into its old ironic lines.

"I'm really too tired to think fast," he said, "but luckily you just handed me an easy one. You do not correct the way I speak to you. Ever. Get the cane. I'm giving you fifteen and then I'll figure out what comes next."

He hit me savagely, and I didn't even try not to cry. And afterward, he just glared at me sobbing and sniffling.

"Just get down on your knees and shut up," he said wearily.

And when I'd clearly done the best I could to quiet down, he began carefully, "What sort of person was he?"

What could I say except the truth? "A...a construction worker, Jonathan."

"Right, downtown buildings," he nodded. "I should have known. But I don't imagine it was your big beefy type. More like a cuddly baby construction worker, right?"

I whispered, "Yes, Jonathan."

"Well," he said, "I didn't say you couldn't, so I'm really not surprised that you did. Would he come here? Would I find him appealing?"

Since I had never even remotely considered either of these possibilities, I had to think hard for a minute. I thought of Kevin's round butt and sweet face and then his hurt and outraged look. The answers were obvious, but it took some effort to frame the simple, logical response.

"Well, yes, Jonathan, I think you'd find him appealing. And, uh, no, he'd never come here." A logical proposition: P and not Q.

He seemed a little miffed by the "never."

"Just good, clean fun, huh? None of this nasty scary stuff for you and your pal the Beaver. Just screwing and cuddling, I guess."

Couldn't he fucking let it alone? No, of course he couldn't. That was the point. I could fuck somebody else, but he had a proprietary right to it, and that was what he was making painfully clear.

"Uh, well...," I temporized.

He looked at me sharply for a moment and considered. "'Well, not quite, Jonathan,' is what I think I hear. Maybe just a hint of kinkiness with Biff or Sluggo or Wally or whatever his name was. Well, that's interesting, anyhow. Maybe even entertaining. I didn't think you'd disappoint me, Carrie."

He opened a drawer and pulled out some hash wrapped in foil and a small pipe. He lit the pipe and took a drag, and then he offered me one as well. I took a meek little toke.

"I've had a grueling, exhausting two weeks, with no entertainment at all, except if you count some old Nina Hartleys on hotel pay TV," he said. "This is exactly what I need. A dirty story. And from such a good talker. I mean, I don't let you talk much, but what makes that fun for me is knowing that you really are a good talker. So talk to me. Tell me the story of you and Eddie Haskell. And remember that I'm not too tired to beat you some more if you skimp on the details."

He sat down and dragged some more on the pipe, like a spoiled little sultan with a hookah, while his other hand unzipped his pants and took out his cock, which wasn't exactly erect, but which looked as though it wanted to be, as he began to stroke it. He held the pipe out to me, and this time I took a healthy drag. Then I settled back on my knees at his feet, straightened my back, and began to tell him a story. Scheherazade.

I didn't skimp on the details, in fact, I juiced it up, timing things better than they happened in real life. I had Kevin unbutton my whole dress with his teeth (Jonathan raised an eyebrow at that one, but let me continue), and I put a lot of energy into describing Kevin's enormous erection and oceans of come. Hell, I thought, if he was going to be so con-descending about "Biff or Sluggo," he ought to be able to deal with that. He winced a bit, but he was pretty high by then, so he decided to find it entertaining—in fact, I noticed he was getting pretty excited himself.

This was certainly the most uninterrupted talking I'd ever done at his house, and the sound of my own voice (combined with the hash, no doubt) was getting me higher than a kite. I started slowing down, putting in more details. I was happy to be able to tell him about the condom, and I could see that he was glad, but he wanted the more hardcore stuff, and I did the best I could with what I had. I sneaked a look at his cock ("eye contact, damn it," he said, smacking my cheek lightly) and wondered whether he'd come before I finished the story—and nastily, I started to try to make that happen. He caught on pretty soon and slowed down his own momentum. And he had pretty good—though not perfect—control, so I got us almost all the way through the handcuffs denouement before he grabbed the ring in my collar and dragged my head down over his cock, coming loudly and drowning the last few words of the story.

After that, things changed between us. Rather a lot, actually. Perhaps they would have anyway, I don't know. In any case, it wasn't just me and Jonathan anymore; now he brought in a whole supporting cast of characters. He spent an afternoon teaching me how to put a condom quickly and attractively onto a guy's cock—I felt like Gigi with Gaston's cigar—and then he started having guests. Some old pals might come over for late drinks and casually pass me from hand to hand as they caught up on old times. Or they might like to lie me down on the floor so that two of them could fuck me at the same time, one in my mouth, one in my cunt. One dynamic duo seemed to have such great synchronization that I figured they'd rowed crew together in college.

Sometimes the events were just that serendipitous, as though it were as trivial to pass a body around as to open a bottle of scotch. But he also liked to dabble in impresario mode, to affect an elaborate show of concern for his guests. He liked, for example, to point out how wet I was inside, how they needn't worry about hurting me because I was already so turned on by my own abjectness. He made me thank them profusely after whatever they did to me. Sometimes he thanked them as well, explaining how much I needed to be used.

I wondered, of course, just whom the charade was directed at. Was it for my benefit? Were these just the next set of lessons in his syllabus, new challenges, new humiliations that I'd think I couldn't bear and then find that I could? Or for his benefit—maybe he'd always been waiting to share me around, as soon as I could be trusted to open all the holes properly. Or was he still pissed off because of the silly Kevin escapade and intent on telling me I was a slut? He was so cool most ways that it was hard for me to believe that he'd much care if I had a minor thing for muscular boys with big dicks and pretty faces. And soon, anyhow, the frenetic pace of these entertainments died down somewhat, and things went back to what I fondly called "normal."

Which isn't to say there weren't still entertainments and events. There were, but they were less frequent and rather more elaborately planned, and easier to accept as events that would turn him on. There might be occasions, for example, like the time he sent me upstairs to one of the guest bedrooms, with a note (written on heavy cream paper) shoved into my mouth. The note, which he gave me to read before he put it into its envelope, said,

Dear Uncle Harry,

Have a happy 55th birthday. Keep Carrie for as long as you want and please don't hesitate to use the riding crop as necessary.

Best regards,

Jon

He had Mrs. Branden tie a big white satin bow around my ribs, with the riding crop placed through the knot at an artistic angle, its loop just brushing my right nipple. Needless to say, giving Uncle Harry permission to use the riding crop was like giving the Republicans permission to cut the capital gains tax. But that was my polite Jonathan, ever the solicitous nephew.

Sometimes he'd bring girlfriends home. No matter what their names were, I always thought of them as Muffy. They seemed to be the daughters of the ladies in the garden-party dresses at the dressage shows. Perhaps they'd be those ladies someday. They were pretty, slender, tanned, and they always had streaky blond shoulder-length hair. And most of them were as cruel as you could possibly imagine, making Uncle Harry look quite gentle and dear in comparison.

I could understand why, though. Here they'd spent this absolutely fantastic evening with this guy who was a great catch (plus fun and sexy and entertaining) and he'd bring them home and want them to make love with his girl slave while he watched. I mean, it wasn't presented that way—at first I'd just be some exotic spice added to the scene, not much more than an extra tongue. They'd be flattered and titillated. But at a certain point he'd draw back, being polite as always, but you couldn't really miss the message—he wanted to watch and he wanted it to be good.

He'd come back in for the last round, of course—send me scurrying away as though somehow it had all been due to *my* randiness, and then he'd do the requisite heroic male fucking number. But it always was a little beside the point, and they knew it. So the evening would end up with them showing me how they felt about it. Jonathan would let them punish me, and they'd really get into it—anything to prove that it had only been *me* who'd been used, and not *them*.

These were the most difficult scenes I had to play, and not just because of the painful beatings. It was the sneaky, fucked-up psychology. I remember the first time I realized that Jonathan was being sadistic, and how silly I felt using that word, under the circumstances. But it was true—I didn't really feel that what went on between him and me was sadism, because we'd, as he'd said, made a deal. But the Muffies were getting something different from what they signed on for, and I thought that was cruel and gratuitous. It wasn't fun for them—all of the other people he threw at me got to indulge their pure and simple demands for obedience, but not the Muffies, who really didn't want me there at all. I wished he wouldn't make me do it; he was showing me a part of himself I really didn't want to know about. Which was part of what I was trying to explain to Stuart the night after Jonathan had told me about ownership and auctions. Although he was as fascinated as I was with the buying and selling part—and especially the big bucks—he was heartbroken that Jonathan wanted to sell me.

"I thought that eventually he'd realize that it was you and only you he loved," he wailed. He was, in fact, deeply smitten with Jonathan, whom he'd finally gotten a glimpse of. We'd been at the Castro waiting for *Les Enfants du Paradis* to start. I'd insisted we arrive early to get terrific seats, and while I was buying us popcorn and the organist was finishing his Edith Piaf medley, segueing from "Milord" to "San Francisco, open your Golden Gate," I spotted Jonathan way in the back and sent Stuart to get a good look. Jonathan was alone, reading something. I don't think he noticed us.

"Yeah, and marry me. Like Mr. Rochester, right? And we could raise a houseful of little perverts. God, Stu, sometimes I think you're in love with him—you're certainly his most swooning and faithful admirer. You deserve to be treated like he treats the Muffies."

"That's avoiding the question," he said. "Are you really going to tell me you started in with him just because you're such a brave adventurer? Didn't you have a big, big romantic thing for him when you met him? At least till you met Uncle Harry, who seems to have changed your life."

"Uncle Tom, Dick, and Harry," I boasted, "and just about every fraternity brother Jonathan ever had. Probably a few who didn't make it into the fraternity, too. And then there's Muffy, Buffy, and..."

"Cottontail."

"Cottontail. Right. The thing is, it really does change your perspective. It's certainly changed my ideas about what turns me on. I think it's the voice. That command voice. Jonathan's great at it, but just about all of them can do it some."

"Except the Muffies."

"Well, that's because of Jonathan's mindfuck. He creates a situation where they can't demand what they want. But even they sometimes hit the voice, sometimes just by accident. The thing I've been trying to explain, Stuie, is that I've

71

started to think of the voice as kind of a transpersonal thing. It's made up of lots of voices. It's beyond Jonathan."

I thought I was being quite impressive, until I heard Stuart snort. "Can it, Car," he said. "I don't believe you. I mean, I can see how it would be a turn-on to be, like, doing it with all of them in front of him. And sometimes, if he's not there, he makes you tell him about it afterward, right?"

"Yeah, sometimes," I said impatiently. "What's your point?"

"Well, it's still *him*," he said. "Muffies or Uncle or whatever, so I don't believe you that it's suddenly so, uh...what was the big word you used, the one that sounded sort of like 'transgressive'?"

"Oh, fuck you," I yelled, suddenly feeling like I was going to cry. "It's *my* damn life, not yours, and I am not going to center it around somebody who, on the one hand, has this strange cruel streak and, on the other, has his life really together and doesn't have to worry about stuff like whether he's really smart or talented or just kidding himself. I mean, he's like fifteen years older than I am—he can probably remember where he was when Kennedy got shot—and he's rich, male, smug, and successful. And I think getting emotionally tangled up with him—like if I cared about that—would be a lot more dangerous than anything I'm doing right now. So fuck you...and...and..."

And I stopped before I could say something like "get a life," which was on the tip of my tongue, but which—given how I'd depended on Stuart this whole year—would have been so cruel and unfair that I never could have forgiven myself. And probably he knew that, since the look he threw me was partly shamed, partly grateful, and also somewhat serious.

"Right," he breathed. "Okay. He's giving you your start, but it's your adventure through life and sex, and he just disappears after a while. That's cool. But aren't you at least sad that he disappears?"

"We'll always have Paris," I said, recovering my equilibrium. "Anyhow, I want to see what happens next. I want that more than anything."

"And how about him?" he asked. "Why does he want to sell you? Is he bored?"

"Maybe," I said, "but I don't think so. I think it's a Pygmalion thing. I think he wants me to go up on that auction block or whatever it is and be the way coolest bottom anybody ever saw. This whole business, from picking me up at the party to turning me into an actual slave and showing me off in public—it's like an aesthetic act. So he's got to complete it, create, you know, closure."

"Aren't you scared?" he asked.

"Stuart," I said patiently, "I am *always* scared."

CHAPTER III

Professionalism

I didn't think Jonathan would tell me any more about the selling idea for a while, and he didn't. Things went on as they had been—quiet days in pornotopia—for a week or two more. And then, late on a Saturday afternoon, when Mrs. Branden led me into the study, Jonathan was already there, drinking wine and talking and laughing with the most beautiful woman I'd ever seen. She was about Jonathan's age and she was, well, perfect. Red gold hair, cut in an achingly pure straight Louise Brooks bob that fell to her jawbone. Big pale transparent green eyes. A black linen suit, tight jacket with no blouse under it, short tight skirt, long, long legs. Decidedly nontrashy red shoes that cost the earth. Short, flawless, bright red fingernails. The little Mercedes I'd noticed parked outside must have been hers, too. This was not a Muffy, and I knew, absolutely—I mean, after all I do know Jonathan very well in some ways—that she and Jonathan had had a wonderful, expensive lunch at some place like Zuni and then had come home and fucked their brains out. It didn't matter that she looked so absolutely perfectly groomed, like she'd been born in that suit about an hour ago. They'd fucked and fucked and then she'd quickly gotten her perfect self all back together again, because that's the kind of person she was.

Was she why he wanted to sell me? All my bravado began to wobble. I was scared and jealous. I tried to look completely compliant and impassive, as I was supposed to look, and I suspected that I wasn't succeeding very well.

Jonathan took the leash and unhooked it, unhooked my hands from behind my back, and did a quick little gesture that I understood perfectly. I kneeled down and kissed her shoe (I knew how to deal with the lipstick by now). Then I stayed on my knees in front of them, staring foolishly at her.

He turned to her. "So, what do you think?"

She laughed a little more and scooped up my chin in her hand, tipping my face up so she could look into my eyes. "Just wait a minute," she said. She had a lovely, husky voice, the kind I'd seen described in some novel as "thrilling." She looked at me hard.

"My god, Jon," she said now, "the little slut seems to think *she* owns *you*. Where's your cane?"

He handed it to her, and she whacked me, really painfully. I started to wail. She slapped me in the face. "Stop that," she said quickly—and amazingly, I was able to.

"Now look, Carrie," she said briskly, "I'm not interested in whatever you think is happening here, so please show a little self-control and don't communicate anything except your desire to obey us." Then she poked the toe of one of her beautiful red shoes into my cunt and gave a witchy laugh. "You're right, by the way, about these. They *are* too expensive, even for me. Now go get that stool." She pointed to a little wooden stool about a foot high, in the corner. "Put it there," she said, pointing to the middle of the room, "and stand on it."

"Yes, ma'am," I said.

"Ms. Clarke," she corrected me, lightly flicking the cane on my ass again.

"Yes, Ms. Clarke," I agreed. Oh Stuart, I thought, scratch everything I said about the voice. It's an entirely different thing when it comes from someone like this. I hurried to do what she said, climbing up on the stool. She stood up and slowly walked around me, looking at me hard, nudging me from time to time with the cane. I tried to interpret her nudges as signals, how to stand better, how to look more graceful. She wasn't very tall, I realized for the first time, maybe even a little below medium height. But you just assumed she'd be tall because she had so much presence. I was very frightened of her, and it took everything I had just to be still. I didn't want her to think Jonathan had trained me badly. Somehow, that seemed very important.

She put down the cane, squeezed my breasts, fluffed my pubic hair. Then she put two fingers in my mouth and parted it a little, while her other hand did the same thing to my cunt. I felt terribly warm and weak. I wanted to come, but I knew that that would be a disgraceful thing to do. I just concentrated on breathing, on not trembling too much.

She let go and walked around me again. "Well," she finally said, "she's pretty enough, just barely. Of course you know that she's not a great beauty, and you also know that in the long run that's what they want to pay their money for. She stands reasonably well, though she's clearly a novice. You could have trained her for dressage, but I know that's not your kind of thing to do. Too bad, though. If she were mine, I'd use a bit and bridle on her. There's just so much training she hasn't had, and it shows. As does her attitude. You're charmed by how bright she is, and you clumsily indulge her, as though she were a precocious child. Sweetheart, are you going through a midlife thing about becoming a daddy? Because we all know that there are pretty girls lined up around the block, each of them willing to tolerate a little, ah, strangeness on your part, in return for marrying you and getting knocked up and putting in an early application at Presidio Hill School. But please don't lay any of that on Carrie, who still, I think, has some decent instincts about elegant sex.

"Because she does have a quality, I'll give you that, Jon. She does have a bruised innocence that some of them will want, and a lovely pear-shaped rump, especially one that marks so easily, never hurt anybody's salability."

He made an exasperated sound. I could see, out of the corner of my eye, that he was simultaneously annoyed, amused, and, despite himself, finding this a big turn-on. "Helluva performance, Kate," he said, dryly, "but is there a bottom line here? Is it a go or not?"

"Damn it," she said, angry but apparently amused as well. "I'm giving you a whole lot more than a performance. I'm giving you expert advice, which would be costing anybody but my oldest friend and lover a thousand bucks. So let me continue, please, too bad for you if I insist on throwing in a lecture. Yes, there is a bottom line here, what a silly term under the circumstances. Yes, somebody will quite probably pay good money for a very badly trained little girl with some evident talent and a pretty body. Not a huge amount of money, but she'll squeak through the trials, and somebody will get a bargain at the auction. Let's hope it's somebody tough and professional, which is what she desperately needs. Still, it's not the way I like to do business, and it's not the way I like to see business done. Why all the rush? Why not train her properly? Why not really develop a product? Send her to me if you're too bored and lazy to do it correctly. Do her good to get out of this misty Wuthering Heights you've got here, anyway. And she'd be no trouble, would you, Carrie?"

I didn't think Jonathan would like it, but I couldn't see promising Ms. Clarke that I'd make trouble for her, even hypothetically. "No, Ms. Clarke," I said.

She laughed again. "In fact," she continued thoughtfully, "Carrie would like to come and stay awhile with me, I think. Not that we—or I, at least—care what she'd like. But I think she's becoming somewhat infatuated with me."

"Bitch," he said evenly. "Well, I'll think about it."

"No, you won't," she answered. "You'll never send her, so don't pretend you will. You will continue in the confused, romantic, amateurish way you've begun, and I will continue to disapprove. At least, though, promise me you'll send her for some yoga or ballet classes. I can see that she's a little jock, but she could really use the strength and flexibility."

She picked up her purse and checked her perfect image in the mirror. Then she put her arms around him and kissed him. It was a long, communicative kiss, seeming to express things I couldn't even guess at.

"Listen, sweetie," she murmured, "I'm sorry I teased you, but you make it so damn easy. God, I miss you, though. I wish we saw each other more often. Even if you won't bring Carrie, you should come to Napa more than twice a year. It's not so far, you know." Her hands, with those perfect fingernails, were all over his ass. He sighed, and they nuzzled a little more. Then they drifted out of the room, arm in arm.

I stood there on the stool, a few tears trickling down my cheeks, waves of shame, fear, and confusion washing over me. I could think of so many things to cry about, I wasn't even sure what was really making me cry. Somebody had betrayed somebody, I thought, but I didn't quite know what I meant by it and who I thought had betrayed whom. I heard her car pull away, and then, about five minutes later, Mrs. Branden came into the study to tell me that Jonathan said I should go home for today.

The next time I came was different, too. Mrs. Branden told me to keep my clothes on — messenger clothes, that day my T-shirt said, WE'RE PRIMUS — WE SUCK — and just to go into the study. Jonathan was standing at a large walnut table by the leaded window in the corner, making neat piles of papers. There was a pot of coffee.

"There you are, good. Listen, this is a terrible pain, but we need to do it together. These are ownership papers, these are auction applications, these are photocopies of the laws that these papers ever so elegantly skate over, so that we can actually be doing this in this day and age. Read everything, then you can ask me questions. Then we can fill them out. Have some coffee. No rules today. I've ordered a pizza and Cokes."

I went back to the kitchen to get my reading glasses — first time I'd ever needed them here — then grabbed a pile of papers, curled up in Jonathan's armchair, and started to read. After a while a pattern emerged.

"It's another virtual reality, isn't it?" I asked, reaching for a slice of the pizza, which had arrived by then.

"Pretty much," he nodded. "There's no real ownership — I mean, how could there be? Just elaborately precise degrees of consensuality and gift giving within the boundaries of international law. Still, the lawyers who wrote these papers were rather talented pornographers and, within the definitions of consensuality, managed to make it sound as though this were the *ancien régime* and the *droit du seigneur* were still a going thing."

"So it's completely legal? And how do they keep it so secret?"

"Probably it could be challenged in court at certain points. But it isn't, and probably for the same reasons that we don't get reporters sniffing around. Most of the people involved in this thing are rich, and some of them are spectacularly, metaphysically rich. I wouldn't exactly say a fix is in, but there is influence at play and payoffs can always be made."

"Swell," I said grimly, "just the crowd I want to hang with. This isn't the part I like to think about, you know."

"I know," he said. "Neither do I. That's part of what Kate means about my being a romantic amateur. She never forgets the bigger picture for a minute."

"So, who is she?" I asked, wiping my mouth. I didn't think he'd really tell me, but I liked to see how far I could go during these little time-out periods when the rules were suspended. And, more than just about anything, I wanted to hear about Ms. Clarke. I could see him start to say that it was none of my business. But instead he took a deep breath.

"Kate? Yes, well. Um. Well, as she said, she's my oldest friend and lover. I mean, we grew up together, our parents were friends, we grew up playing sports and playing doctor. I'm a year older and Kate is about a decade tougher. I honestly can't remember a time when I wasn't sexually involved with Kate, if just at the level of peeking and groping. And then a whole lot of early teenage experimentation. First just screwing, hours and hours of it, but then we discovered pain, and power. Domination, control. Together, I mean we just sort of stumbled into it, maybe because being so close made us so brave and foolhardy. Or maybe, really, it all came about because Kate was gutsy enough to demand what she wanted, in so tough a voice that it scared us both, and started us thinking about a whole other level of desire and expression. Whatever it was, when we got started—God, it was like two teenage science prodigies setting up a lab in the basement. And practically blowing up the house. We did some ridiculous and dangerous things. I've got scars. I guess you've seen them."

"Yes," I said wistfully, just about dying of awe and envy, "I have. Uh, who's, who's...?" I found myself asking the question, but then I couldn't get the words out.

But he was amazingly forthcoming. "The top, you mean? Well, me, for starters, of course. I mean, we read *Story of O*, too. But then we read a lot of other stuff, we tried lots of stuff straight out of the books. *Venus in Furs*, naturally. Even Bataille, though we really didn't get more than sticky with eggs and milk. We played from lots of angles, lots of roles. All in all, it was pretty polymorphous-perverse, and it still is, which I guess is what you really want to know about. I mean, we don't use hardware at all anymore. It's more like that joke about the prison, where the prisoners know all the jokes so well that they just call them out by number and everybody laughs. Kate and I know so many of the same scenes, and we know each other so well, we can run lots of different and contrasting scenes very economically in a short time, just out of fucking and eye contact."

She dumped him, he said, just before his senior year in high school. He was stunned. He had thought they'd be together forever. "Together how?" she'd asked. "With our parents buying us the big spread down the road? *Owning* things together? Uh-uh, sweetie." It took him awhile to figure it out, but it wasn't quite so terrible when he realized that they could still fuck from time to time.

"And then, when I was at college, I got to go to a slave auction, for the first time. Uncle Harry took me. And there, on one of the little pedestals, was Kate. She was supposed to be at Sarah Lawrence, but she'd somehow engineered this stunt. Her parents found out afterward, and there was a big stink, but it was too late then. She was a sensation, of course, brought in more money than anybody had before. She got famous in those circles, wound up running a remarkable establishment in Napa with maybe the most gorgeous slaves in the world."

"She's the one with the poker games, right?" I said. "I would like to see it sometime, you know," I added.

"Forget it," he answered quickly, and rather grimly. "I've changed my mind about that one."

I was surprised. I guessed I had overstepped some mysterious boundary. He looked a little frightening. He lit a cigarette, and I hugged my knees to my chest in the big armchair. We both were quiet for a while. Then I almost whispered, "Jonathan, am I really so badly trained?"

"That's a tough one," he said. "Yes, I guess so, I guess by Kate's standards you are, but Kate's standards are astronomical. For God's sake, a lot of this is sensibility, after all. And anyhow, there are different standards, different games, different coordinates for plotting reality. I, for example...oh come on, Carrie, if we can talk about Kate we can talk about this—don't play dumb. You know very well what I'm talking about, even if we've never talked about it before.

"The game we play is objectification, right? You are what I want you to be, or you get thrashed, as you well know. Of course, we both know that there's got to be a 'you' to actively 'be' what I want you to be. But there's no simple reversal. There's something I can only call originality, your jagged little edge of critical intelligence that could go home and turn this all into a story and write it down. It obliterates itself at my command and then what's weird is that I feel as though I'm compelled to search for its trace. The story is written somewhere under its erasure, maybe. Or something like that, like something out of that god-awful fancy frog theory you read so much of at school. Ridiculous, obscure, pretentious, but still…it seems to describe something that's really happening. Something about the ass-backward way, excuse the expression, in which we—all of us—feel and perceive and communicate. I mean, here I am, not even letting you speak most of the time but still straining to hear it, that calculating, deadpan, cranky, comic narrative little voice saying, 'And *then* Jonathan said…' and making me sound, oh quite sexy, but just a little ridiculous and full of myself too. Anyhow, that's what interests me. It's pretty elusive."

"Gosh," I said. It was about all I could think of to say. "I didn't know you thought about stuff like that," I added. I was pretty blown away. I certainly hadn't been playing dumb. I had genuinely *been* dumb. I had been playing so hard, so sincerely (his word), that I seemed to have missed a whole level of the game.

"I know," he said. "You wouldn't. You're not quite open-minded enough to expect stuff like that from somebody as boozhie and mainstream as I am. Still, I try. I read a lot. I read what I think I need to read to understand what I want to understand. It doesn't match your "Masterpiece Theatre" image of me, but there it is."

"I've got to think about this some more," I said slowly.

"That's exactly right," he said. "You do. You're a kid, after all, and sometimes I forget that. Sorry. Really, I mean that. You know a lot more than you think you know, and I know you think about it a whole lot, but you haven't really thought it through. After all, it's a shocker, and a blow to the ego, to consider that sex might be as difficult and complicated as literature."

I was beginning to wonder if these seemingly ruleless sessions were where he scored his biggest points off me. Perhaps the rest of the arrangement he and I had wouldn't work without these talks.

"It's getting late," he said. "We should get back to work."

"No," I said. "Because even though this is important stuff, you haven't really answered my question. Am I so badly trained that I'll be in big trouble out there, wherever it is?"

"Now *that's* disingenuous," he said. "You know there's no answer to that question. I'm not training you for 'out there.' Even up to the last day, I'm training you for me, and don't you forget that. Of course you're going to wonder about 'out there,' but really, you'll just have to wait and see, won't you? I'm not saying that we shouldn't be paying attention to some technical things. Kate's right about ballet and yoga and so forth, you can start going next week." He handed me some more of those little business cards. "And I think you should

84

quit your job and move in here. The auction is in six weeks. Let's finish these papers. But first, I have a question for you. What are Primus?"

The next weeks were tough and scary, as you can imagine. No more palling around over pizza, and it about broke my heart to pack up and say good-bye to Stuart. Still, it was clear that if I was going to do this thing, I'd have to stop being a part-timer.

And anyhow, all of a sudden Stuart was hardly ever home. Because Stuart was in love. So he was at Greg's house, or at the library studying across the table from Greg, or maybe he and Greg were working on an AIDS crisis line somewhere, or just sitting on the couch holding hands—all that good stuff, I thought, and felt a twinge of loneliness, as I rang Jonathan's kitchen doorbell, carrying only a small suitcase and a backpack with a few books in it and my huge desire to find out what would happen next.

It was a whole new ballgame, the intensity, the inexorability, and yes, the boredom of it, the fact that I was on call twenty-four hours a day, except for the welcome relief of the ballet and yoga (and they were tough too, though I was sure Kate was right—they'd come in handy). I slept on a little pallet next to Jonathan's bed, chained to the headboard. I served his meals, on my knees. In fact, there were days when it felt like I never got off my knees. He used me as a footrest, an end table, an ashtray. He cut short his work at his office, bringing projects home, and I spent some excruciating times staying as still and quiet as I could and waiting for him to look up from his work—his papers, drawings, or the CAD program on his Mac—and command me to lick, suck, spread, or

open. There were days when I wasn't allowed to say anything, days when I couldn't use my hands for anything, doing
everything with my mouth. I'd learned the original rules quite
well, but now there were always new rules, new reasons to
punish me.

One of the most intense changes, I realized, was not
having any money. I mean, I did, really. I had a bank account,
with a little bit saved from my job. But Jonathan had me sign
it over so that I couldn't get at it, at least until after the auction if I didn't get sold, or until I was free, if I did. It was a
very lucid contract, written by one of the pornographer
lawyers, and given the small amount of money involved, it
couldn't have been worth what Jonathan must have paid him
to write it up. But like all the other stage props in his virtual
reality, it did its job. Especially in contrast to how I'd felt
zooming around downtown on my bike, I felt profoundly
unfree.

Jonathan or Mrs. Branden would give me money to get
on the bus to go to ballet or yoga, and to come right back
home after the lesson, which I always and unfailingly did.
There was a great grungy coffeehouse right downstairs from
the ballet studio, too, where I would have loved to hang out
with a book and a latte, if I'd had the money for a latte. I'd feel
like the little match girl, practically pressing my nose against
the window, staring at all the normal people at the tables. And
then I'd get onto the bus going home, reaching into my pocket
for the exact change. Kevin was right, I'd think. Carrie, you
are weird.

I'd feel tired, melancholy, disoriented, and a little
scared, as the bus strained uphill to Jonathan's neighbor-
hood. And then, little by little, I'd start feeling really hot. The

bus would be chugging and I'd be sort of taking inventory of my body. I'd feel the newly stretched muscles, the welts and bruises. And my wet, warm insides. My jeans and sweaty leotard would begin to feel foreign. I'd think ahead to taking them off, to bathing and drying myself and making myself up, and then silently presenting myself to Mrs. Branden to be cuffed and collared, perhaps shod and corseted. I always shuddered, and probably always would, when she'd buckle the collar in place. And no matter how good my posture was getting, how straight my back, how strong my belly muscles, the collar would transform me. My head would lift, my breasts would thrust, filling me with a sense of how tender, how hurtable they were. I would, in that moment, feel myself become an object—his object, only better than an object, because I had a consciousness and a will and an intelligence that I would knowingly hand over to him. And then it would be free fall, the moment after I'd given him my center. I could feel myself preparing for that moment, that moment when he'd only look at me, for what would feel like hours, until he could tell that my body was begging him to touch me, any way, any way at all.

How could the people on the bus not know this about me, I wondered. Couldn't they smell it or something? Perhaps they could. Perhaps, I thought, they'd go home tonight and surprise their bored and tired spouses.

So, really, Jonathan's little lecture about my critical intelligence didn't really make much difference in practice. I did like thinking that I was making him a gift of my smarts and wit—rolling it up in a ball and tossing it to him to play with or throw away, as he chose. But except for those sweaty bus rides, I didn't really think much about it. Time hurtled on. Jonathan seemed compelled to plumb the depths of his inventiveness; and all the new rules and rough strife, I just kept trying my damnedest to learn and to obey.

Well, maybe once it made a tiny difference. One day he showed me a dress he'd had made for me—gorgeous, black, very short, and backless, with a high jeweled neck that looked like a collar. "Oh, Mr. Rochester," I said—it just popped into my mind and I couldn't stop myself, and I guess somewhere I knew he would think it was funny. He did, too. He was amused and then mightily pissed off when he realized that it was going to be difficult to hit me hard enough for that transgression and not have any stray marks show outside the boundaries of the teeny dress. He managed, though, and I very seriously considered whether I was ever going to try to be even mildly funny again.

Then he had me put on the dress. Underneath, I was wearing a corset and black stockings, with a new, Conan the Barbarian of a dildo belted firmly up my ass. "We're going to the opera," he said. A big limo came to the door. We got in; he sat on the seat and I knelt on the floor and sucked his cock the whole way there while he sipped champagne, and then I had to sit through the whole fatuous opera performance—*The Abduction from the Seraglio,* I guess that was his idea of a joke—with my lipstick smudged and my mouth full of the taste of him, feeling utterly riven up the ass and helplessly exposed (the audience was full of nasty Muffies), while he watched me smugly.

At intermission, he pulled me to my feet while most people were still applauding. I hoped that this meant we could go—maybe he wanted to play some more in the limo—

but really I knew better. He led me to a central area where people were buying drinks and sitting down with them at tables. It was already crowded, with people dressed every possible way, and buzzing with all kinds of chatter, but he found us a table. He leaned across it and said very softly, "I'm glad you gave me cause to beat you earlier. I like knowing how bruised you are under that pretty dress. Makes you seem more naked. It's difficult, isn't it, being so near to naked in the middle of this scene."

"Yes, Jonathan, it is difficult," I replied. Bastard.

"Good," he answered, almost gloating, but maintaining his stuffy schoolmaster voice. "Now, I want to see you on your hands and knees, here, in this room. Do the best you can. I'll be over there by the wall."

"Yes, Jonathan," I breathed. Oh yes, Jonathan, swell.

The best I could think of was to drop an earring and get down to retrieve it. Pretty tame, but given the shortness of my dress, pretty difficult too. Looking at nothing at all, pretending a kind of idle calm, I fiddled with the post of my left earring, slowly wiggling it off, being careful to keep it folded in my hand. I kept my head very still and the earring stayed in place. Then I moved my head slowly to look at Jonathan, leaning against the wall with his arms folded, watching me intently. Well, I thought, if he knows about my bruises, I know about that hard-on that's starting up over there, as I glanced at the area of his loose Italian suit that wasn't hanging exactly as Giorgio had intended. Then I raised my eyes to his, to catch his wry little look of "touché," and my earring fell to the floor at my feet.

What would I have done, I wondered, if it had rolled all the way across the floor? But it hadn't, so I slowly got down, keeping my eyes locked to his. I'm just retrieving an earring, I kept repeating to myself, trying my damnedest not to feel too obvious and humiliated in the middle of this shrine to cultural excess and obsession. At the same time, I kept hearing his tone of command and my own tone of obedience, his "I want" and my "yes, Jonathan," the duet playing on some internal radio that seemed always to be turned on whenever we were together.

Down on the floor, I simply posed for an instant, all meekness and compliance, eyes on his, mouth slightly open. Okay? I wondered, and then, suddenly and joltingly, found myself staring at him as though I had never seen him before. Nothing like being in a crowd of strangers to hype up the familiar a little. I guessed that was what he was enjoying as well. It made me a little dizzy for a moment, and then, mercifully, my head cleared. Ready or not, I'd been down on the floor quite long enough, I thought, and grabbed the earring.

I got up slowly, being careful not to let the dress ride up too high. I felt like a diver surfacing. All of a sudden, I was aware of all the chatter around me again. And, miserably, uncomfortably, I was also aware of several pairs of eyes on me. Just how conspicuous had I been, I wondered? There was no way I could know. I tried to screen the stares out of my consciousness, to disconnect from the lines of force that the gazes described. I knew that if I looked I'd see the kinds of questions that I had seen before in people's eyes, on the rare occasions when Jonathan and I had been together out in the "real," nonpornotopia world. I mean, we were hardly blatant or anything, but face it, we'd always get some attention. At first, naively, I'd thought that was because he always saw to it that we wore such great clothes. But it wasn't, of course. It was that, for those with eyes to see, there was always something extra, some buzz between us, some way that he'd hold my arm just a little too tightly. Somebody would always notice, some eyebrow would always be raised. The clash of our private virtual reality and the real world was deeply disturbing to me, and he was a genius at exploiting my discomfort.

So as I got back into my seat at the table, I wasn't entirely surprised to see a very queer looking man, dressed all in black with steel-rimmed glasses, raising his champagne glass to me. I got flustered and turned my head away, and my eyes met those of a little girl, maybe eleven years old, her pale face surrounded by unruly curls, in tacky dark green velvet with a white lace collar. Her gaze was calm and steady. I didn't think that she understood. But I knew that she *knew*. Oh, what the hell, I thought, and returned her gaze. Don't be scared, it's just what it is, I tried to communicate to her. Life is really surprising. She seemed to absorb that, not really to understand it, but in the way of wise children, to file it away for when she'd be ready for it. She's smart, I thought, a whole lot smarter than I am—and I put on the earring, jamming the post tightly.

Jonathan strolled over, finally. Cheerfully, he kissed the top of my head. "Not bad," he said. "You were a little rude for a moment back there, but you already know that. We'll deal with it later, of course. Anyhow, not bad, not bad at all." He lifted me by the elbow and led me back to our orchestra seats. I could feel a run snaking down my stocking. He'll like that, I thought. I hardly heard the rest of the opera.

Afterward, he punished and then fucked me in the limo, parked at the top of Twin Peaks, while the driver watched silently through his mirror. And when he'd driven us back to the house, Jonathan asked if he'd like to have me suck him off, as a tip, he said. Of course it really wasn't a tip — Jonathan just wanted to see what it felt like to watch through the mirror — but I don't suppose the driver cared about making such a fine distinction. Anyhow, they traded places, and they both got what they wanted, and then Jonathan also gave him some money as well as the leftover champagne, before we walked back into the house.

CHAPTER IV

Kibbles and Bits

A few days after our night at the opera, the phone rang in
Jonathan's study. He picked up the receiver, listened
for a minute, and started talking loudly. "Doug, that's ridiculous, the ventilation works fine, it's a minor adjustment that
I've planned for already. No, they don't need me. I can walk
them through it over the phone, I don't have to be there for
the whole damn week while they install. Because I'm busy.
No. No, personal things. No, I can't tell you."

He waited a bit, pushing me off his lap to a kneeling
position on the floor, then rubbing my head distractedly. They
were probably putting him on a conference call; his quality of
life would take a turn for the worse, I thought, when those
things all had video components built in.

Anyway, he argued with Doug, and then Doug and Stan
and Carol, for about fifteen minutes, speaking that horrible
singsong whiny yuppie-ese he could do so well: "But we've
already *completed* that deliverable, Stan," and "*Yes*, Carol, I
understand that your comfort level is not high." And by the
end of it, he'd promised to go to Chicago the following
evening, though he was adamant that he was right and they
were wrong and that it was stupid for him to go. But the deal
was that he'd walk them through the installation, whatever
that was, in person, and then he'd be entirely done. No more

calls, and no way were they going to mess up his trip to Europe in ten days—that was the auction, though of course they didn't know it.

I figured I'd finally get to go to Chicago, though I didn't really see that fantasy making much sense at this point, or how he'd fit it into our current intensive training schedule. But just then an alarm went off on his Mac to remind him that it was time for me to go for yoga, so he unbuckled my collar and shoved me out of the room.

He was very quiet and intense that evening, though, and didn't mention any changes, not that I'd expected him to. In fact, he was oddly affectionate, if you can call fucking me just about every way possible affectionate. I was exhausted, nearly swooning; though he did beat me, it was rather lightly, with his belt, before he sent me to bed early.

The next morning, however, after I'd brought him breakfast and eaten some myself at a plate at his feet, Mrs. Branden brought a man I'd never seen before into the study. He was different from anyone I'd ever seen visiting Jonathan, I thought. He was fat and late-fiftyish, in a buoyant, Sydney Greenstreet kind of way, and he wore corny light blue polyester pants and a yellow alligator shirt. Jonathan had me kiss his shoe—white loafers!—and called him "Sir Harold." Oh, right, I got it. This was one of his porn movie friends, or something like that anyhow. One of those silly-looking guys he respected so much. Well, the man was for sure silly-looking. As for what this was actually about, well, we—or I, really—would just have to wait and see. Not that there was much I could do about it anyway.

He sat down in Jonathan's armchair. Jonathan sat in the straight chair opposite, and I knelt at attention, my shoulders in front of Jonathan's knees. Mrs. Branden brought in coffee and rolls. Sir Harold dunked his rolls, wolfed them down, and talked. He was expansive, affectionate, fatherly almost, toward Jonathan, and Jonathan was very, well, respectful. There was some chatter about "business," about how the good old days were, of course, better than these benighted times, about how Kate was doing in Napa. I couldn't tell much from the conversation, until finally it seemed to turn to the matter at hand, which seemed to be me.

"Anyway," Jonathan was saying, "it's wonderful of you to help at such short notice. I would have had to take her with me, which wouldn't have worked out at all, or send her to Kate."

"Would've been fine to send her to Kate, you know," Sir Harold rumbled, finishing the last of the rolls. "Don't know why you're so set against that."

Jonathan winced. "Well, she's busy. She's got some big deal going this week. Some emir or a senator, or both maybe, I don't know."

"Don't give me that, Jon," the fat man said. "Kate can always handle one more little girl, no matter what she's got going. You don't want to send her, fine, I'm glad to help. But that's your call. Anyway, let me have a look at her."

Jonathan patted my shoulder. "Stand up, Carrie," he said. "Let Sir Harold look at you."

I stood up and walked over to where Sir Harold was sitting. "Turn around, girlie," he said. I did, slowly.

"Legs look okay," he said. "Rides a bike, you said? And ass, too. Well, more than okay, poetic, even. Kind of ass that talks to you across a crowded room." Block that metaphor, I thought, and I could see that Jonathan was a bit nonplussed by it as well, even as he nodded, somewhat shyly.

"How's the mouth?" Sir Harold continued.

"Pretty good, I think," Jonathan said. He'd regained his cool. "Try it, why don't you? Kneel down, Carrie."

"Unzip me, girlie," Sir Harold said, "and put it in your mouth." His cock wasn't totally erect, but it grew, rather spectacularly, as I sucked on it, and he pushed, insistently, for the back of my throat. He made some guttural, moaning noises, but I could tell that he was seriously checking me out all the while. I could tell that Jonathan was nervous. I did the best I could, though I was nervous myself. What was all this about?

Rather than come, though, he pulled out and grabbed my shoulders. "Turn around," he said roughly, pushing me as he said it. He was very strong, and his big hands were very sure, and he quickly had me turned around with my ass up. I was surprised, but Jonathan clearly wasn't, because he was ready with the ottoman. And when I was quickly positioned on it, he parted the cheeks of my poetic ass himself.

Sir Harold finished fucking me up the ass, groaning and bellowing. It hurt, and I had tears in my eyes by the time he was done, but I figured I'd done all right, whatever that might have meant.

When he'd pulled out of my asshole, and was zipping himself up, relaxing, and catching his breath, Jonathan signaled to me to return to my original kneeling position, at attention. I did, and both of us waited silently a few minutes, our eyes on the fat man in Jonathan's armchair.

"She'll do," Sir Harold finally said. "You've taught her a few things, I guess. I'll take her with me."

Jonathan made a relieved sound and bent to kiss my shoulder blade. "Get a coat, Carrie," he said. Take me with him where?

When I had put my coat on, and some shoes as well, we walked out to the front of the house. There was a pickup truck parked there, and attached to the back was one of those carrier vans that they use to transport horses. You know, you see them on the freeway sometimes. They're usually somewhat open, so you can see the back part of the horse, but this one was closed over. The shape was the same, though. On the side was lettered SIR HAROLD'S CUSTOM PONIES. My knees began to wobble, and I wanted to turn and run, but Jonathan put a hand at the small of my back, steering me toward the curb at a steady pace.

Sir Harold opened the back of the van, so we could walk in. There was room for the three of us, since the van was made to carry a horse. We stepped onto clean straw, heaped on the floor, and he closed the door behind us.

"Strip," he said to me, "and then bend over."

I handed my coat and shoes to Jonathan. The straw under my bare feet was disturbing. I bent at the waist, holding on to a horizontal bar in the front of the compartment. I could feel a greased dildo probing my asshole. I took a deep breath and Sir Harold shoved it all the way up, belting it into place with stout brown leather straps. And then I could feel a tickling against the backs of my knees and thighs. Hair. It was a long horsetail, attached to the end of the dildo. Sir Harold slapped my ass. "Up," he said.

He fit a set of narrow straps over my head, buckling it in back. One of the straps bisected my face, down the middle of my nose, and two more angled down from the top of my nose practically to the bottoms of my ears. Together, they held a hard plastic bit in place in my mouth, stretching it widely and making it impossible for me to speak.

"May I see her, sir?" Jonathan asked timidly. Sir Harold nodded and slapped my ass again, indicating, I realized, that I should turn around.

Jonathan stared raptly at me, as though he'd never seen me before. He stroked my breast softly and then rubbed me behind the ear as though I were an animal, to be communicated with in this way. It was unbearably humiliating, the bit making me mute, the tail making me less than human. I clenched my bare toes against the straw and looked at him miserably. He continued to stare at me, one hand on my ass under the tail, the other touching my face through the straps. I lowered my eyes, but he slapped my breast hard, and I knew that meant he wanted me to keep looking at him. They'd speak to me, I thought, as little as possible while I was, as I realized, a "custom pony." I raised my eyes, sighing and shuddering a bit.

"You're making her skittish," Sir Harold said, stroking my ass slowly with one of his big, meaty hands. Amazingly, his stroking did seem to calm me down. "Quiet now, quiet now, that's it," he crooned to me. They *would* speak to me, I corrected myself, but only like this, a kind of brief, phatic communication meant to elicit a physical rather than a verbal or cognitive response.

Sir Harold turned to Jonathan. "She's a nice bit of flesh, see, but high-strung, like you. It'll take some work, you know." He attached a set of reins to brass rings at the ends of the bit and tugged. The pain in my mouth was echoed by stabs of feeling in my cunt and breasts and waves of shame. I remembered wondering how this would feel. It was new, and very frightening. I turned in the direction of the tug, away from Jonathan and toward the front of the carrier. Sir Harold attached the reins to the bar that I'd been holding. Then he nodded to my hands, and I held the bar again. I figured I'd need to do this in order to keep my balance once we got going. He attached the rings on my cuffs to rings on the bar, on either side of the ring where the reins were attached. Jonathan stroked my ass one more time.

"In a week, you won't know her," Sir Harold was assuring Jonathan as they stepped out of the carrier and shut the door behind them. Would I know myself? I wondered.

The pickup truck's engine started. I held on tight. Pretty soon we were on the freeway, crossing the Bay Bridge. There was a little round window I could look out of at my side. At first I was frightened that people could look in at my bridled face, but passengers in cars didn't seem to see me—not even little kids, who were staring extra hard, trying to get a glimpse of the pony. Finally I decided, with some relief, that it was a one-way window. Probably it looked dark or like a mirror from the outside.

I didn't have a watch, of course, so I don't know how long we were on the freeway. Two hours, maybe? And the little window wasn't really angled to let me see the road signs. All I knew was that it was hot and sunny outside—I could tell by the bright sun through the window and the warm air coming through the vents in the carrier. From the little I could see, it looked very rural outside—we were somewhere in the Central Valley, I supposed. The ride became bumpy as we pulled onto a gravel road, and bumpier after Sir Harold unhooked some gate and we went uphill for a few minutes on dirt and stones.

Finally we stopped. He came back into the carrier and, wordlessly, detached me and led me out by the reins.

I blinked in the brilliant sunlight, stepping onto a patch of grass. A young man in jeans, cowboy boots, and an Aerosmith T-shirt was holding a pair of sturdy, thick-soled lace-up boots in his hands and grinning at me. He had dark skin and very white teeth, I could see as my eyes adjusted to the light, and he knelt to tie and buckle the boots onto my feet.

"Not bad, boss," he said. He was short and solid, the T-shirt stretched against a broad hard chest and shoulders. "No experience, though. That's pretty clear. What's her name?"

"It's Carrie," Sir Harold said. "We'll put her next to that blond, curly-headed one. Hey, is she named Carrie, too?"

"Cathy, boss," the young man said, grinning again. He seemed easily amused. Maybe working all day with naked girls in bridles and tails had always been his dream job. The boots were tightly laced on my feet. They felt solid, making me want to stamp my feet. The young man gave my pubic hair a friendly little yank and then got to his feet. We were standing near a fenced-in ring of ground, maybe thirty yards in diameter, and he looped my reins over the fence.

Within the ring, maybe half a dozen girls, bridled and tailed like me, were going through various paces, supervised by a few guys in jeans with riding crops in their hands. The girls were all doing different things, so it was hard for me to get a fix on the general principles involved. One was jumping hurdles. A few others were practicing various gaits, walking, trotting, and a kind of slow run—a canter? Two were harnessed together, trotting in what looked to me like perfect precision. Another was goose-stepping. Yet another was marching, her knees very high. Unlike the rest of the girls, who wore boots like mine, she wore very high-heeled shoes. I winced as I watched her feet move over the uneven ground.

Just then I heard quick footsteps and a jingling sound. I turned in the direction of the sound and there it was, the whole deal, the finished product, coming down a path toward us from some rolling wooded hills. If they'd wanted me any more agitated than I was now, they couldn't have done better at that very moment than to show me this.

It was a cart, a small one-seater on two large wheels, designed a bit like a plough, or a backward wheelbarrow. There was a man sitting in it, holding reins and a whip, and, running quickly but carefully, lifting her knees elegantly in front of her, a harnessed and bridled girl. Her bridle looked like mine, and the man in the cart was holding the reins. I couldn't entirely make out the complicated arrangement of other straps that attached her harness to the cart, but I could see that her cuffed wrists were hooked to metal handles, which were like the handles of a wheelbarrow, and that this was where a lot of the pulling happened. It was, all in all, a simple but fiendish little contrivance, and it seemed to work well. I mean, they were going fast, and as they approached us, I could see that she was sweating and breathing hard and that the man in the cart was smiling broadly.

They weren't seeming to slow down as they approached us, and I figured they'd just go past. In fact, I could hear the crack of the whip as the man used it to speed the girl up. But just some twenty yards from us, he pulled hard on the reins, jerking her head back cruelly. "Whoa," he yelled, "whoa, Stephanie." And she dug in her heels and stopped, almost on a dime, I thought, pulling up so close to us that I could see that her eyes were a violet blue.

The man jumped out of the cart, looping the reins over the fence not too far from me. I stared at Stephanie curiously.

101

The bridle distorting her mouth and the dusty rivulets of sweat running down her face and body didn't stop her from being supernally beautiful. She had long black hair, and to keep it from getting tangled in all the straps, it was done in a thick braid, near the top of her head, coming out through the straps of the bridle. But tendrils and curls were escaping everywhere, and you could see that when the braid was undone there'd be oceans of gorgeous black curls. They'd cascade almost to her perfect ass, crisscrossed with whip marks and bisected by a tail like mine and over her goblet-shaped breasts, which were heaving as she panted. Her peachy skin was flushed bright pink under the dust. I kept looking at her, transfixed, but she just looked straight ahead, consciously evening her breath, stretching and relaxing her muscles.

Aerosmith undid all the straps and buckles that attached her to the cart and then began rubbing her down with a soft cloth. When she was dry, he stroked her ear a little, crooning gently to her, "Easy, easy, goo-ood girl," much as Sir Harold had done to me in the van. She seemed to need it a lot less than I had, though. Her breathing had quieted down and evened out, and she looked calm and serene — well, bored, actually. Aerosmith patted her breast — she looked off somewhere into the middle distance — and he sighed softly, took her reins, and led her down a path to some barnlike buildings, downhill from us. They disappeared into one of them.

Meanwhile, Sir Harold went to talk to the driver, a Mr. Finch, I gathered. Though Mr. Finch clearly had had the time of his life cracking the whip over Stephanie's bouncing ass, you could see that the experience wouldn't be complete for him if he couldn't find anything to complain about. Still, all he could come up with was a small squeak in one of the wheels and his wish that the weather were not quite so hot. Sir Harold nodded sympathetically, with the easy confidence of a tradesman who has utter faith in his product. He opened a small compartment at the back of the cart and pulled out an oilcan, oiling the offending wheel until the squeak was entirely gone, then putting the oilcan back.

The cart, I could see upon closer inspection, was no glorified wheelbarrow. Though I figured that its body was actually made of some kind of light fiberglass, it was covered with a molded wood veneer and painted a glossy black with red and gold detailing. The spokes of the wheels were also gold, and the seat was soft dark red leather. There was a little brake apparatus over one of the wheels, I realized—otherwise, it would have run Stephanie over when she'd stopped so short. It was skillfully and practically designed, but it looked like a tiny fantasy coach, reminding me of fairy tales.

Sir Harold was telling Mr. Finch that in the future, if he heard a squeak, he should use the oilcan himself. Each cart, not to speak of each pony of course, he repeated a few times, got a thorough going-over between rides, but you never knew.

"It's a tough job," he sighed, with some relish, "old carts, new ponies, always something needing my attention. Like that one over there, by the fence, fresh and green and unbroken. Took her on as a special favor to her master, nice boy from the old days. She'll be all right, but she'll take some work. You get to know the signals in my line of business. Nice body but likes to think too much. Not like that little Stephanie, who responds to the slightest tug, and you just lay the whip on for the pleasure of seeing the pretty marks."

Speaking of Stephanie made Mr. Finch remember that he'd also paid to be blown by her and that she'd probably be cleaned up, groomed, and ready for him in the stable by now. He shook hands with Sir Harold and hurried down the path.

Sir Harold gave me a long look. It was the first time I'd been alone with him, and I realized that he frightened me intensely. He was onto me, I thought. He knew that, at least at first, I wouldn't be good at this, that I need words, not strokes or slaps, to make me obey. He wouldn't tell me anything directly—nothing meaningful, anyhow—but he'd managed, through his little speech to Mr. Finch, to communicate all this to me. I returned his look solemnly, trying to communicate that I understood what I'd have to work to overcome, and he nodded briefly, so I guess he was satisfied.

"Frank," he now yelled, to one of the guys in the ring, "take this new one, name's Carrie, down to the stable. Put her next to Cathy, feed her, and give her a nap. We'll start training her this afternoon."

Frank was tall, rawboned, freckled, quiet, friendly. I guessed they'd all be friendly. He picked up my reins and slapped my ass. "Nice girl," he said briefly, "come on."

We walked down the path at a good clip and entered the barnlike building I'd seen Aerosmith lead Stephanie into earlier. It was a stable, divided into stalls on both sides of a center aisle, with straw heaped on the floor. It didn't look special in any way—I mean, I don't think it had been built for girls being treated like horses. I think it had, at one time, actually held horses. Maybe the only modification was that the door to each stall was just high enough so that it came up to your neck. And they must have cleaned it out with great care when they'd converted it. It didn't actually smell like a stable, but it did smell, a little—of straw, and of, well, of flesh, I guess. I counted seven stalls on each side.

We passed a stall where I could see Mr. Finch's shoulders and the back of his gray-blond head and hear his moans. I could also see a chain attached to the stall's back wall, trailing down the wall and onto the ground. The chain was moving rhythmically, and I knew, even though I couldn't see her, that attached to its other end, in the straw on the floor of the stall, was Stephanie on her knees with Mr. Finch in her mouth. And I realized that part of me was glad she was having to blow this unpleasant guy—gorgeous snooty perfect little bitch. Dumb, Carrie, I thought. Before you're out of here, you'll probably have to do a lot worse. But I couldn't help what I felt.

Frank let me into a stall and quickly took off my tail and bridle, as well as my collar and cuffs, which I'd been wearing all morning and which came from Jonathan's house. He hung the tail, with its straps and dildo, on a hook on the wall and then took all the other hardware somewhere else. I wondered why he'd taken the bridle. Then he came back, took off my boots, slapped my ass again, and nodded to the door of the stable. I followed him out and he led me a little further down the path to an outhouse, a regular one, only rather large, with room for maybe a dozen people and no seats, just holes in the floor to squat over. It was quite clean for an outhouse, which is to say, just a few flies.

When I'd finished there, he led me back into my stall and put a loose chain collar around my neck, hooking it to a long chain attached to the wall at the back of the stall, like the one I'd seen in Stephanie's. Whistling as he did all these chores, he went out again and returned with a pan of food and a little trough of water, both of which he attached to the top of the door of the stall, so I could eat and drink standing up (and of

course not using my hands), facing the stable's center aisle.
The food was a grain and vegetable mixture, tasting vaguely
of oats, but formed into little pellets like breakfast cereal.
Science Diet, I thought, specially balanced for girl ponies.
The only pieces of the food that I actually recognized were
the cubes of raw carrot and celery mixed in with the kibbles
and bits. I hadn't realized how dehumanizing it would be to
eat food that had been prepared entirely for its nutritional
value. I didn't want to do it, but I was hungry and figured that
I'd better. And when Frank came back holding a large, perfect green apple, it looked so appealing to me that I ate it out
of his hand and, after he'd tossed the core, licked his sticky
fingers clean. He stroked my head, to dry his hand, and then
my face, and it frightened me that I was beginning to feel a
kind of affection for him.

Then he came into the stall, stroked my ass, crooned to
me that I was a good girl and needed some rest, and pointed
to the pile of straw with some blankets on it. I crawled
between the blankets and fell asleep.

When I woke up, it was a lot busier in there. There were lots
of girls in the stalls. I guessed they'd given me an early lunch,
because I was new, and I'd been asleep when the rest of
them had come back. And now they—we—were all getting
out again. The stable guys were busy bridling and harnessing.

Pretty soon one of them, one I hadn't seen before, came
in to get me ready.

"Back to work with you," he sang out, "up, up, thatta
girl," as I stumbled to my feet and rubbed my eyes. He reat-
tached my tail, first regreasing the dildo. Then he put a
different bridle on me. It looked the same as the first, but the

bit was cold metal. I guess the first one had just been for practice. He took off the chain collar and put a harness arrangement around my torso. It buckled over my shoulders and ended in a new, stiff, collar. There were also matching cuffs, which he hooked together behind my back, up a little above my waist, so they wouldn't be in the way of the tail. Then he put on my boots again, attached some reins to the bridle, and led me out of the stall.

As the business of the afternoon unfolded, I figured out that there were four guys working fourteen girls in the stables. There were Frank and Aerosmith, whose name was really Mike, and two others, Don and Phil. The four worked well together, yelling questions and answers to each other, sharing tasks. And they were fast. I mean, putting all the hardware on us was no loving B&D ritual; it was a job they were paid to do, like sweeping out the stable and greasing the wheels of the carts. It probably took Phil about as long to do up all the straps and buckles and laces on me as it has for me to describe him doing it. And this included a once-over, after he finished, a general straightening and tightening of everything, until I felt almost corsetted. Leading me out of the stall, he went along the center aisle, stall by stall, and gathered up a bunch of other girls' reins in his hand. So there were four of us that he was briskly leading down the path back to the ring, the midafternoon sun making everything look lovely, golden, and pastoral.

Walking fast to keep up and trying to find a comfortable way to rest my tongue against the bit took a lot of my attention. So it took me a minute to notice that one of the other girls Phil was leading was gorgeous Stephanie, just floating along, her tail bobbing. I tried to make eye contact with her, and when she clearly, if subtly, refused, I felt myself involuntarily rolling my eyes and sighing behind my bit. I doubt that I was audible, but my body language must have been expressive enough, because the girl on my other side bumped her hip against me, and when I looked at her, she nodded toward Stephanie and did a perfect matching eye-roll.

I would have smiled at her, if the bit had let me, and I guess she could tell that. As we hurried along, I got a chance to look at her. She had short, curly blond hair, a pointed chin and high cheekbones under the straps of her bridle, very firm conical breasts that her harness caused to jut way out, and great, lithe muscles under lovely suntanned skin. Cathy, I guessed. And she looked familiar. Now where had I...well, the body remembers, even if the mind is overwhelmed by new rules and concepts. Involuntarily, I found my eyes moving to her thighs, searching for the marks. And yes, there they were, very light, almost, but not quite, healed and still unmistakable, those evenly spaced marks. I remembered her mistress from the dressage show and Cathy's worshipful look. I was glad, though, that worshipful as she'd been there, she clearly had a sense of humor. Even if all we could do was roll our eyes at each other, I was glad she was here.

By this time we, and the groups of ponies led by the other guys, had all reached the ring. Sir Harold was there, supervising busily, and the guys were really hopping. Some of the ponies were being harnessed to carts—I noticed there was a two-seater, to be pulled by two ponies harnessed together, and even an elaborate little open coach, to be pulled by two pairs, one in front of the other. I would have been fascinated to watch the intricacies of the harnessing arrangements, as the nicely dressed folks waiting to drive were doing, but Frank led Cathy and me into the ring, with a sharp tug on our reins.

He led us to a corner where there was a sort of maypole arrangement with chains maybe ten feet long dangling from the top. A circular path had been paced into the ground around it. Looping our reins behind our backs, he attached a chain to each of our collars. Then he positioned us carefully at points in the circle around the pole, Cathy at twelve noon, me at three o'clock, both of our chains standing tautly out from the pole. Loudly but curtly, he barked out, "Walk!"

And we did. I tried to copy Cathy exactly, her speed, her posture, and I was careful to keep the distance between us constant and the chain taut. You would think it would be a piece of cake, and I actually thought I was doing very well, but damned if Frank's riding crop didn't keep falling on my calves, or my ass or shoulders, almost every time I passed him. "Head up!" he'd shout. "Tits out! Knees higher!" and damned if he wasn't always right, too. Cathy's head would be held higher, I'd realize after the fact, her body more complexly and elegantly displayed than mine. Drooling behind my bit, I put everything into trying to get this together.

I must have improved somewhat, because we advanced to trotting and cantering (I guessed goose-stepping was part of the advanced course). And I felt like I was really improving when, as the afternoon wore on, the times I didn't get hit started to outnumber the times I did, even though Frank was barking out his commands with great frequency, making us change gaits almost in midstep. I could relax a little, I realized, just enough to realize how painful and difficult this really was. The muscles in my legs ached, and my back and my belly too, from holding myself up so perfectly straight as I circled around and around. And the accumulated bruises and welts from the riding crop began to hurt more and more. Dusty, salty sweat was dripping into my eyes, I was panting, and a little drool was running out of the corners of my mouth.

Finally we stopped, and Frank wiped the sweat off us while we cooled down. It had been hours, I realized, hours of painful, monotonous walk-trot-canter. The weather was still warm, but the sun was a lot lower in the sky than it had been when we'd started.

Sir Harold and our guy from this morning came over to where we were standing. The guy unhooked Cathy from the maypole and led her away, and Sir Harold said to Frank, "Let's see what you could do with her." Frank commanded me to trot, and I was off.

It was harder to do without Cathy in front of me, but my muscles seemed basically to remember the rhythm. Frank kept quiet and let Sir Harold bark out corrections and lay his riding crop on me. He hit harder than Frank, of course, but even he didn't hit every time I went around, so I figured I was ahead of the game. And when I stopped, and he curtly told Frank to clean me up, adding, "You can have her if you want," I knew I hadn't disgraced Frank or myself (or Jonathan, I surprised myself by thinking).

Frank quietly led me back down to the stable. I saw that most of the other ponies had already been taken back and been cleaned up. The only ones left in the yard were some girl who was still being dried off and Stephanie, whose hair Aerosmith was lovingly brushing. That hair, I thought, God, it must take hours of their time to wash out the dust and brush out the tangles. Still, Aerosmith looked like he was in heaven (it didn't look to me like this was just a job for him, and I wondered how he could stand it), and Stephanie, once again, looked like she wasn't here at all.

Frank took off all my hardware, putting it in a neat pile on the ground. Then he turned a spigot and aimed a hose of cold water at me. I gasped. I hadn't expected that. The water pressure was hard against my bruises, though nice against my sore muscles, as he thoroughly soaped me down head to toe with a soft brush and then rinsed and dried me.

"Okay, okay," he sang softly to me, picking up all my straps and other assorted hardware, "back in your stall, just a little more work this afternoon and then you get a nice dinner." He slapped my ass and I hurried in, wanting to get both the work and the yucky dinner over with and just collapse in the straw.

He came into the stall with me, hung all the hardware neatly on its hooks, attached the chain collar, and then surprised me by kissing me on the mouth, a long, deep, tonguey kiss, that made me moan and kiss him back. "Pretty mouth," he murmured, "so pretty without its bridle, oh yes…"

And then he surprised me some more by whispering in my ear, "And forget about this stupid horse thing. For the next little while you're a girl, not a damn pony."

Then he went over to the straw and lay back, leaning on his elbows, sticking a piece of hay between his teeth and jerking my chain to pull me along. He pushed my shoulders down to the floor so that I was on my knees, and lifted one of his feet. "Now, darlin'," he drawled, "you can use that pretty mouth to clean my boots."

Oh yuck. His old cowboy boots, leather and snakeskin, were covered with dust and dirt and pieces of grass and hay. I thought of licking Jonathan's meticulous shoes, of that first silly little humiliation when he made me lick the lipstick off. Welcome, I thought, to the great outdoors, city girl.

It took awhile—quite awhile—to clean off those boots and my mouth really tasted awful, when I'd finished. Frank gave me some water to drink, and then he undid his buckle and pulled off his belt.

"Now suck me good," he said softly. "You treat me as good as those boots, Carrie, or I will whale hell out of that little ass, and not with a riding crop, but with my belt, maybe with the buckle end."

If I was a girl, I figured, I could use my fingers to unzip his jeans and take out his cock, and I thought I'd test these new, local rules a little. So I whispered softly, "May I use my hands to take out your cock, Frank? May I touch it with my hands?"

He grinned and cuffed me lightly, "Polite, aren't you? Well yes you may, darlin', if you hurry the hell up."

So I did. I unzipped him, fished around just a little until it practically jumped out of his pants, and sucked and sucked, while he grinned and moaned, his big hard hand on my neck.

After he came, rested for a while, and put his belt back on, he jerked the chain attached to my collar and whispered, "Pony time." And then we were back to the pony game, me standing quietly at the stall door and him whistling, patting me, and crooning animal inanities as he got me some more healthy Science Diet for dinner. And as I crawled between the blankets on the straw, hoping my sore muscles would get rested enough overnight for whatever was in store tomorrow, I wondered just how many levels of mindfuck I'd have to deal with in this place.

And then, just as I was about to drift off to sleep, I noticed a really odd thing. A little piece of rubber hose, maybe two inches of it, was snaking its way through a knothole in the wall of my stall, the wall, I realized, that I shared with Cathy. And softly but unmistakably coming out of the hose was a whispering sound, "psssst," to get my attention.

I put my mouth to the hose and whispered, "Cathy?" and then put my ear to it.

"Yeah," she whispered back. "So, what do you think? What was Frank like?"

"A pervert," I answered. "He likes to talk to the ponies as if they were girls."

She stifled a giggle. "I caught some of that. Sir Harold sure wouldn't like it if he knew."

"How'd you get the hose?" I asked.

"Yesterday, or day before," she answered, "they had me crawling around the yard with a little saddle on, and I found it on the ground and palmed it, just in case I got a neighbor I wanted to talk to."

I felt like a new kid in summer camp who had just made a best friend. Life was looking up.

Cathy had been here for four days and would be here another three before Madame, as she called her, picked her up to take her home.

"She's thinking of showing me at those dressage shows," she said, "so she sent me here to get some basic training. She may put in a ring, all that stuff, at her house. Hire a trainer, even."

"How do you feel about it?" I asked.

She surprised me, then, by a total transformation of her whispered voice. The bratty, giggly tone disappeared completely, and she answered simply, "I'm honored, of course. I just hope she'll be pleased when she sees what I've learned."

I didn't know what to say to that, so she continued, "And your master—he's the beautiful man with the gray hair, right?—why did he send you here?"

I explained, as best I could, about my training for the auction being interrupted by Jonathan's trip to Chicago. She knew about the auctions, but not much more than I did.

"But to have to leave your master. I'd die if it were me," she said. "How did you displease him, Carrie? Isn't your heart breaking?"

I was pondering how to answer all this when we heard footsteps. One of the guys was coming through, doing a bed check, I guess. I snuggled into my blanket and pretended to be asleep. And the next thing I remember is waking up the next morning in a pool of bright sunlight.

Feed, groom, harness. The routine really wasn't going to vary, I realized. My leg muscles were stiff, but not horribly so, and when the guy—it was Aerosmith this time—came to put on my bridle, boots, and all the rest of it, he skillfully rubbed my calves with some stuff out of a brown bottle, which seemed to help.

When they'd gotten us down to the ring, they harnessed me to a cart. This one, however, looked a whole lot more like a wheelbarrow. I mean, it was clearly a practice cart and might as well have had a sign on it that said STUDENT DRIVER. Still, I stood very straight as Don pulled the straps tight and attached the rings in my cuffs to the cart handles. Then he came up to me and silently showed me the whip he'd be using. It was long, braided, scary-looking dark brown leather, and he looped it in his hand, stroking my breasts, my pubis, my face through the bridle.

Finally, he climbed into the cart, pulled the reins, and yelled, "Walk!" I started up and soon came to a fork in the road. It was easy to tell, though, that he wanted me to turn right by the sharp tug on the right rein, so I did, and we were off, soon trotting along what looked like a pretty hiking trail, up and down hills, through copses and over ridges. When he wanted me to change gaits, he'd yell that, but he'd also accompany it by a coded set of tugs and pulls on the reins. And after about half an hour, he stopped yelling anything, just testing me on my understanding of the tugs and pulls, and flicking the whip over me whenever I was slow to get a signal. It was difficult. I was scared I'd lose my footing, step into a hole, or turn my ankle on stones in the path, particularly as I ran down the steep downhill slopes.

And when I began to feel a little more confident about where to place my feet on the path and how to understand the signals, he started laying the whip even harder. Because it wasn't enough to follow instructions, keep up a steady clip, and keep my balance. I had to look good, keep my head up, tits out, knees up, ass bobbing. Well, what did you think, I chided myself, that the folks who'll be driving you will be paying Sir Harold for a look at the pretty countryside? And I found myself flashing on mental images of racehorses, their snorts and the angles of their heads, and the fastidious ways they placed their hooves. I tried my damnedest to look good, and I began to feel a perverse pride in it all.

We were back on open, level ground now, heading, I guessed, back toward the ring. We turned a corner in the path, and I realized that we were heading straight for a low stone wall. I wasn't getting any instructions to slow down from Don — had he fallen asleep at the wheel? Hey, I might be perverse but I'm not crazy, I thought, and began to prepare for a halt, when all hell broke loose. The reins jerked my head back, the whip started raining down on my shoulders and ass, and Don started shouting insults, "Bad, bad, no! Bad pony! Stupid girl!"

I stopped running — the reins were certainly telling me to do that now — and he jumped out of the cart and ran up to me in a fury. "Did I tell you to slow down?" he yelled. "Did I tug the reins or yell to slow down? What the fuck made you think you could decide that? What the fuck made you think at all?"

Of course. The wall was supposed to be a test. And I'd flunked immediately. After the fact it seemed so simple. Of course they wouldn't let me go into the wall, and they did not fall asleep at the wheel around here. Don would have jerked me to a halt in plenty of time, I realized. I was stupid. And bad. I hung my head and wept in front of him.

He watched me for a while and then slapped my cheek lightly. "Head up," he said, but not unkindly. "We'll try it again."

He got back into the cart, reined me around, and we went back a few hundred yards along the path. And this time I just kept running toward the wall, proudly and trustingly, until at the very last minute he jerked my head back and I dug my heels in and stopped — well, I stopped every bit as short as Stephanie had done the day before. And as we trotted back to the ring, which wasn't far from the stone wall, I was delighted by Don's murmurs of praise and encouragement and almost ignored the thought that crept unbidden into my head just then: Sir Harold was right; Jonathan won't know me.

Don reported to Sir Harold that he thought I could pull paying customers now, giving him the specifics of the morning. Sir

Harold looked almost convinced and said he'd think about it, and Phil unharnessed me and took me back to the stable for grooming, food, and a nap. And that afternoon, I got my first paying customer.

Given my luck, of course, it turned out to be a Muffy. I mean, not one of Jonathan's Muffies, just a specimen of the generic type. Which means, even though I think I did reasonably well, I got hit quite a lot. I think that there's something about me that gets to them, that I'm a symbolic stand-in for themselves, for their fevered imaginings of how they'd do in my place.

But then, as Sir Harold said, I think way too much. I'll never be able to change that, but I realized that first afternoon that I was learning how to keep it at bay while I was pulling a cart. I mean, there's just so much physical data to have to deal with—the light, shade, and colors whizzing by, the shape of the path under my feet, the complicated embrace of the bridle, tail, and harness, the pleasure and desire of the driver, translated into tugs at the reins and slaps of the whip. Then there are the ache of my own muscles and bruises, the pounding of my feet and heart, the sharpness of my breath in my chest, and the burn of salty sweat dripping into my eyes. And the challenge, the ceaseless challenge to look good, proud, upright through it all.

Well, wax poetic over it as I might, my new pony persona didn't stop me from gossiping and giggling with Cathy through the hose after dark. It was a nice break, a way to be myself. But not too much myself, or too deeply. Because I discovered that although Cathy liked nothing better than to talk endlessly about Madame, her elegance and her cruelty, I didn't want to talk about Jonathan. I was confused about what I felt about leaving him.

And Cathy was cool. She didn't understand me, but she did understand that each slave was unique in what made him or her tick, and she stopped asking me things I clearly didn't want to answer. So we just used the evenings to compare notes, on customers, on the stable guys—especially when, as bonuses for extra good work, Sir Harold let them use us—and of course on the other ponies. We pieced together the information that while most of us were temporary boarders, our masters and mistresses doubtless paying obscene sums to Sir Harold for our training, Sir Harold owned four girls himself. Those were the ones who could goose-step, or even, Cathy whispered to me in awe, negotiate the path through the woods in heels. I found this difficult to believe, but I watched them whenever I got a chance, Gillian, Cynthia, Anna, and Jenny, and they were so astonishingly surefooted, so proud and gorgeous, that I thought maybe it could actually be true.

But our favorite topic of bitchy gossip was, naturally, Stephanie, nasty little good girl princess Stephanie. Because even Sir Harold's ponies didn't have her haughty manner, her way of doing everything perfectly but of not being here at all. It was as clear to Cathy as it was to me that Mike—Aerosmith, as I still thought of him—was pathetically infatuated with her, and we didn't approve of that. All the rest of us had figured out a kind of rapport with the guys who worked for Sir Harold, an admiration for how good they were at their jobs, and a sympathetic acceptance of their idiosyncrasies (like Frank's girl perversion). It was amazing how much you could express with a bit in your mouth, and how much people communicated to you, I thought. And I remembered, with a start of recognition,

Kate Clarke's telling Jonathan that if I were hers, she'd put a bit and bridle on me. She'd been right, I thought, I had needed this training badly.

Stephanie, though, it was as though she didn't need this training, as though she were above it. Cathy and I were as nasty and bitchy as we could be, egging each other on to imagine humiliations for her, humiliations she never got, of course, because she was so prissy and perfect. If we'd been in summer camp, we would have short-sheeted her bed by now. Or dipped her hand in a bucket of water while she was sleeping to make her pee in her sleeping bag.

"What I would have liked to see," Cathy whispered one night, "was her pulling a plow." It was her last night here — Madame was coming for her tomorrow. She was so excited that she couldn't sleep, and I was so sad about her leaving that I couldn't, either. So we both were overtired and punchy, repeating all our old Stephanie jokes just for companionship. But this plow stuff was news to me.

"A plow?" I whispered. "They have a farm here?"

"Well," she answered, "when Madame drove me up here, on the road through the grounds, we passed a girl pulling a plow. They have a vegetable garden, I think, and they grow some flowers. Anyhow, the girl, she's gone home since then; she was all tired and muddy and everything, and, you know, bent over. She looked terrible. Madame asked Sir Harold about it and he just rumbled, 'Punishment.' And then he looked at me and said, 'For a pony who didn't behave.'"

"Wow," I breathed, "it does sound terrible; it would be perfect for her."

And we were so taken with this image, both of us, that we didn't even hear when Phil and Mike, both of them that night, came through for a bed check and shined a flashlight right at the rubber hose between my mouth and Cathy's ear.

"Well," Phil drawled, "will you look at this? Two little ponies talking on the telephone. Or pretending to talk, anyway, because everybody knows ponies can't talk. Why, that's so cute, Mike, I think we'll just have to show the boss. Get the fuck up, you two."

And while we scrambled to our feet, he and Mike gathered up all our hardware in our arms — boots, bridles, everything, and not forgetting our telephone. Then they each grabbed a riding crop and began hitting us hard, on the ass, driving us barefoot through the night, running up a path we'd never been on to Sir Harold's house.

It was an old-fashioned house on a hill, with a porch around it, gables and gingerbread and cupolas. There was a light burning in an upstairs window, so it wasn't long before Sir Harold came down to open the door, barefoot with bony, hairy ankles and wrapped in a voluminous maroon bathrobe with a big gold crest on the pocket. He nodded as Phil explained the situation and showed him the little bit of hose, which he put in his pocket.

"Talking to each other," he murmured. "Shocking. Well, boys, we've got a busy night ahead of us. Get the two-seater out and harness these bad ponies to it. I'll be down in a few minutes."

Phil left to get the two-seater, while Mike started getting us into our harnesses, bridles, tails, and boots. I was scared by the idea of a night ride — and of the fact that I doubted that this would be our only punishment — but I was even more afraid to look at Cathy. She was sobbing silently, huge tears coursing down her face, and I knew that she was thinking about Madame coming tomorrow. Sir Harold would doubt-less tell her everything.

It couldn't have been more than five minutes before Mike returned with the two-seater cart and attached us to it snugly. Then Sir Harold floated down his front steps in shoes and socks but still in his bathrobe, carrying a large, menacing black whip. He shot us a fearsome look, climbed into the cart, and cracked the whip over us, pulling the reins to signal that we head out for the path over the ridge and through the woods, and at our fastest gallop.

And that's all that happened for the next hour. We ran and ran, faster and harder than I could have imagined, the whip cracking over us, both of us groaning, weeping, pant-ing, and feeling as if this would just go on forever. Once in a while one of us would slip—the path seemed different in the dark and sometimes in the thickest parts of the forest you couldn't even see the moon—and the other would have to drag her along until she got back into the rhythm. Once we both slipped, just about at the same time, and I thought dimly how lucky we were that we were going slightly uphill, so that the cart didn't just roll over us, because I didn't trust Sir Harold to use the brake. We staggered to our feet, the whip blows raining down on us, and started up again, and maybe ten minutes later, Sir Harold drove us back to the ring, where Frank, Mike, Don, and Phil were all sitting on the fence, waiting by the light of a Coleman lantern.

"I want them back at my house in an hour," Sir Harold said, as Don and Phil jumped down to unharness us. "You boys can have 'em till then." And he hiked up the path to his house on the hill, his robe billowing behind him.

They took everything off of us except our tails and pushed us into the ring. Then, slapping our asses hard, Don said curtly, "Run!"

I couldn't see which direction Cathy was running in. I just started running, barefoot, in the direction the slap seemed to be telling me to go in. And I got about halfway across when I felt a rope around me, pulling me to the ground. I looked down at myself, puzzled, to see a rough rope looped around my torso, and then I looked up, to see the other end of the rope in Frank's hand. Lassoed, my god, I didn't know these guys could do rodeo tricks. Which is what they did for about fifteen minutes, all of them taking cracks at roping us, pulling us down hard, reining us in.

Finally, they seemed to be tired of that one and it was Mike, I guess, who yelled at us, "Get down on your hands and knees and look at us."

And when we did, in the center of the ring, he added, "You two look disgusting." It was true, too. We were a mess, filthy, sweaty, wet with tears and drool.

The other guys nodded, and Phil added, "If we wanted to fuck you, we could wash you down. But that sounds a little too much like what we do on the job every day—the boss just throws in the fucking so's he can get away with the pitiful wages he pays us. And you know how damn hard we work. So, no, working's not what we have in mind. We were thinking, more like, of watching."

And then they were all very quiet, waiting to see what we'd do. And I looked at Cathy, and she looked at me, and bruised, miserable, exhausted, and scared as we were, we had to smile a little. I mean, these really weren't bad guys and it really wasn't the world's worst punishment they'd cooked up for us.

"Uh, well, could we wash ourselves a little first?" I asked. "Or, each other?"

"I guess," Frank said grudgingly, "but hurry up."

One of them threw us a rag, and we ran to a spigot near the gate of the ring. And we got a little of the worst sweat and crud off each other. And I kissed Cathy softly on the mouth, and she stroked my breast a little, and then we came back, hand in hand, to the middle of the ring.

Where we just stood, looking at each other and considering. I knew that the guys were starting to get restless, but I figured we were entitled to think about this for a minute. Then Cathy took a step forward and pressed her front against mine. We were pretty much the same height and I loved how her breasts felt against me. I started to rub, started to paint designs on her with my own breasts, up and down and around. She was firm and smooth—sandstone, I thought at first, an Eskimo carving, but getting warmer and softer and more yielding every minute.

She pushed me down to my knees and I licked the shape of her concave belly, the ridges of her hipbones. I made huge circles with my tongue, stopping just short of her pubic hair, while my breasts ground into her thighs and my hands grasped her ass.

Until finally she couldn't stand being teased by my mouth any longer and pushed my head into her crotch. "Fuckin' A," I heard one of the guys mutter, and I realized that they'd gotten off the fence where they'd been sitting or lounging and were clustered around us. Good, I thought, maybe I'll teach them something. I mean, it wouldn't hurt things around here if they ate a little pussy, now and again. And I dug my tongue in and explored, tracing the shape of her labia, then settling in to suck. I heard her moan and felt her short, sharp orgasm. Fast, I thought. Shit, I paid too much attention to the guys and not enough to her. I looked up at her, expecting some mild disappointment, but was surprised by her intent look, her shining eyes. Like, I thought wildly, a vampire in the moonlight?

But no, this story does not make that wild genre switch, it just modulates, ever so slightly, as Cathy did, pushing me to the ground and lying down next to me. And kissing me deeply, while her fingers opened my vulva and entered, moved, clenched, and moved some more, and…oh my god, I felt knuckles. My eyes flew open and I saw her green-brown eyes and wicked smile, and I remembered that I'd admired the muscles in her arms. Biceps, triceps—the girl was wasted on a pony farm, she should have been pitching the World Series. Or so I thought, when she gave me a chance to think at all, just banging me, wide open and stuffed full, while also never so aware of the horsetail dildo up my ass, crowding things up even more. I came and came and it didn't seem as though she would ever stop. I realized that I was going to have to beg her to, which I didn't really want to do, but what a joke, me and I'm sure also the guys thinking that they were in for a show of some girlie lingerie sex, even if we were rolling around in the dirt, and getting this instead, and to hell with it, I'm not proud. Stop please! Cathy, beautiful Cathy, I beg you, thank you.

"Ohhhhh," I groaned. And pulled her down and kissed her. And she whispered, "That was new for you, wasn't it? I'm glad it was me, then."

And then the guys were all over her. I was scared for a minute, not knowing whether they were going to gang-bang her or what, but it turned out they were more interested in high-fiving her. And I couldn't imagine why she'd worry about Madame, who, it seemed to me, would be so horny after a week away from that genius arm that she'd care less about a little length of hose. I mean, she might be cruel and elegant, but she probably wasn't stupid.

Still, it looked like our hour was up, and Don and Phil walked us up the hill to Sir Harold's, rang the bell and waited in the hall after he'd pushed us into a little office he had. He told us to get down on our knees in front of his desk, while he sat on the edge of it, swinging one leg. And then he took the little length of hose out of his pocket and just asked quietly, "Which one of you?"

And you know that he thought it was me anyway, and that I figured he might as well keep thinking it, because Cathy was looking scared again of Madame, and, well, I didn't know what Jonathan would say or think about any of this, so I figured I'd risk it. That was how I finally ended up spending the rest of that strange night wrapped in a ragged blanket in a tumbledown little shack next to the vegetable garden, trying to get some sleep before I had to wake up the next morning to pull the plow.

It was actually dark when a rooster woke me up. I stretched and groaned. Everything hurt, especially my insides, and I wondered if Cathy had pulverized them beyond recognition. Cheap, I thought, at the price.

Because I was realizing that even as grubby, achy, and unsure of what the day would bring as I was, I was downright cheery. When you've been *that* massively fucked, I thought, life just doesn't look so bad. I looked at the filthy little hut

I was lying in, the hairy, greasy rope looped around my neck and tied to a hook in the wall, the dirt under my fingernails and on just about every other inch of me, too, and I shook my head in disbelief that I could actually be feeling anywhere near good. And then I shrugged, turned over, and got another half hour of deep, dreamless sleep.

When I woke up again, it was to some nasty kicks in the ribs, which I realized had been probably going on for some time. "Up, now, you lazy thing, get up *now!*" I heard. Right, okay, yeah, lazy thing, that's me, I thought groggily, okay, how do you want me? I figured I'd try hands and knees, which would take less effort than any other position I could think of. And I guess that was right, or close enough, because the kicks stopped.

I looked up at a heavy, round-faced woman, dressed in overalls, work boots, and a floppy sun hat, holding a pan of what looked like garbage. Table scraps, I realized, as she put it in front of me. And tastier, once you got over the weird feeling, than the Science Diet they'd been giving me in the stables. I nosed out a little slice of salami—pepperoni, actually—and thought, it could be worse, Carrie.

I was worried that I'd start to annoy the woman if I continued to be so cheerful. Hell, I was starting to annoy myself. But she really didn't seem interested in my mood. She gave me some water to lap and then told me to stand up. But I couldn't. At least not all at once. My bruised muscles just didn't want to. They kept trying to fold back up, like cheap lawn furniture. The woman looked on stolidly, and when I could finally stand straight, she silently led me out of the hut by the rope, after having picked up my bridle, harness, and tail.

126

She put them on me (I guessed I'd have to go barefoot), and then she strapped the harness to the plow, which was just standing out there in the middle of a half turned-up field. No stroking or crooning at me, that was for sure. And then she grabbed the reins and briskly began to lead me down the rows, occasionally swatting me with a thin stick she held in her other hand.

And that was that. I mean we just kept going. Back and forth as the sun rose in the sky and sweat started pouring off me. It was hot, hard, and boring. It was work. It didn't have the little gut-wrenching thrills of exposure and humiliation I had come to expect — I hadn't realized just how much I'd come to expect them. The woman hardly looked at me, and I had to admit that it was a hell of a lesson and a punishment, kind of a metahumiliation, being out there dirty, naked, exhausted, exposed, and virtually invisible. I remembered Jonathan, that first day in his study, asking me if I liked to be looked at. Had it really been so obvious?

From the field, I could see cars coming and going down to the stable area. Customers, of course, but it was also Sunday, and Cathy'd told me that "Sunday to Sunday" was the customary term for a boarder. So Sir Harold had really done Jonathan, that nice boy, quite a favor by taking me on in the middle of the week and driving all the way down and picking me up, too. I wondered, idly, about just what had gone on in the old days, while I watched a beautiful, expensive car drive up the road toward the gate. Briefly I caught Cathy's rapt, triangular face at the window and Madame behind the wheel. And then they were gone and the woman was swatting me to hurry me up. So now I was naked and invisible and lonely as well.

The field I was plowing was, of course, bare, being turned over for new crops. But there was a field opposite where they were growing vegetables and some flowers, and there was also a greenhouse. You could walk down a path between the fields, and once a couple came that way to buy flowers from the greenhouse, the woman just leaving me to stand around while she helped them. The couple chattered happily as they walked away with their flowers, and it was so silent out there, except for an occasional car on the road and the slap of the woman's stick on my calves, that I could hear them even after the path curved away and I couldn't see them.

The voices faded eventually, and then I heard some new voices, new people coming my way. And realized that these voices were familiar. I heard Sir Harold's rumble first, though I couldn't quite make out his words. And then another, a woman's voice that was unmistakably familiar and melodious, the words quite clear as the speakers approached.

"I'll have to give her to the emir tonight. It's his last night, and he's been drooling over her photographs. He'll love the job you've done on her. It's just that she's so unmarked... No, it's not your fault, darling. You were the good girl I've taught you to be, and Sir Harold just couldn't find enough reason to punish you. But we'll beat you when we get home, just to put some lovely marks on you."

And as they came into view, Sir Harold and Kate Clarke, with Stephanie between them, unbridled but harnessed to a little wicker cart, Stephanie said softly but joyously, "Yes, Kate."

Filthy and sweaty as I was, they seemed like creatures from a different world—Kate in a short, crisp, pale yellow sundress and wide straw hat; Stephanie, her eyes never leaving

128

Kate, looking like an adoring child with her hair in two pony-tails over her dazzling naked shoulders and breasts; and Sir Harold decked out in a silly blue blazer. I looked down at my bare dirty feet and I wanted to disappear into the earth.

I should have known, I thought. A slave as beautiful and perfect as Stephanie. I remembered Jonathan saying that Kate's standards were astronomical, and now I knew what that meant. I felt that up until this moment I'd simply been pretending to play a game I didn't understand at all, one whose rules and parameters were written in a complicated and impersonal, perhaps mathematical, language. I realized why Stephanie hadn't cared what went on here, except, of course, for learning to be a perfect pony. For Kate. All for Kate. I wondered if I'd ever be that kind of slave, worshipful, adoring, and totally without irony. I wondered if I wanted to.

Kate was coming over to me, having sent Sir Harold and Stephanie to the greenhouse to get flowers. The woman left me in the half-plowed row as she hurried to help them. I watched Kate walk carefully through the plowed field, her perfect sandals somehow managing to stay clean. But she wouldn't touch me, would she, I thought. I mean, I was too dirty, too abject, for that. And I realized that I wanted, more than anything, for her to touch me, any way she would deign to.

She was smiling at me, almost triumphantly, even as she looked at me with her hard, appraising stare. And then she amazed me by coming very close and softly stroking my breast.

Very quietly, she said, "You are very much improved, Carrie. Even if you didn't steal the little hose — and I don't think you did — you needed this punishment. And this week.

The world is a lot larger than Jonathan's precious little study, isn't it?"

I nodded, tears in my eyes, as waves of sensation rippled from my breast down to my knees. I didn't so much understand her meaning as feel it, glimpsing a never-ending horizon of pain and challenge, as yet unimagined extremes of experience opening out for me, if I were brave enough to try to encounter them. If they were what I really, really wanted...

And that was all. Sir Harold and Stephanie came back, Stephanie's wicker cart piled high with sweet peas and snapdragons, and Kate joined them on the path back to the stables. I just pulled for the rest of the day, numbly, barely noticing the little Mercedes leaving the ranch an hour or so later, mostly keeping my eyes on the hard, bright sky, on the hawks circling in the distance.

They brought me back to the stables that night, washed me down, and put me to sleep, and the next two days passed uneventfully. The pony routine was simple and challenging, and I was open and pliant whenever anyone came to the stables to use me. Sir Harold, I could see, was surprised at how well I was doing. He hadn't expected me to be able to get beyond my intellect as well as I had. What he didn't understand was that at that moment the weirdness of my situation had simply undone me. I would have been happy to forget my surroundings, knit my brow, and meditate on what in the world was happening to me, but it was all too much for me, so I just let it go, half believing that I'd never lived anywhere but in a stable.

Besides, I realized suddenly, as I saw Jonathan coming down the path with Sir Harold, it had been Jonathan who'd kept me so cerebral. He'd never entirely let me relax into the fantasy—he wasn't a master I worshiped, the way Cathy clearly did Madame, or Stephanie Kate. He was a "master," surrounded by ironic quotation marks. He was also Jonathan—neurotic, compulsive, a control freak firmly rooted in the obnoxious world of conference calls and deliverables. Somehow he'd managed it so that I never forgot that about him—we'd played a double game out on the edge the whole time. Or further out than the edge—this was the moment, I realized, when Wile E. Coyote looks down and realizes that he and the Road Runner are standing on thin air, five feet off the cliff, and fifty feet above the ground.

He was coming toward me and all I could think of was what I'd miss about him. Not, I thought, his tone of command or assurance—hell, I figured I'd find that wherever this adventure took me. What I'd miss were the little, funny, off-center things: a raised eyebrow or an ironic grimace, the hair on his belly, the bones in his wrist. And gestures, especially his defensive gestures when I'd caught him out as middle-aged or otherwise unhip. I'll miss, I thought, all the "gotcha's"—undercover ways we'd teased each other beneath the stately minuet we'd been dancing all these months. And I knew, no matter what I'd thought we'd been doing, and no matter what roles we'd been playing, what a joint feat of the imagination it all had been. Even if I'd thought I was in free fall all that time, in another way we'd certainly been collaborators. A collaborator, I thought, remembering when he'd sent me for that first haircut. Oh my.

He and Sir Harold were standing in front of me now, Sir Harold asking him whether he'd want to take the long path or the short one, and whether he wanted to harness me to the cart himself. I was shocked, somehow. I hadn't realized that he'd drive me. Well, of course, I answered myself, I mean, wouldn't he want to see how you've done here? But he seemed a bit hesitant himself, finally agreeing to the short path, while he harnessed me up every bit as quickly and tightly as Don or Phil could have. And I ran through the woods as quickly and gracefully as I possibly could, and he used the whip sparingly, though he was good at cracking it, and at driving—he seemed to know the paths. In fact, we didn't even use the whole path; he turned off at a shortcut and we were back within twenty minutes.

Nobody was around, as he undid all the straps, taking off the harness and bridle, kissing me briefly, rubbing me down carefully and silently. I wasn't supposed to say anything, of course, but I had the idea that he didn't know what to say, either. I mean, what was there to say except something like, Here we so beautifully are, mission accomplished, over and out.

Sir Harold was hurrying down the path now, panting and surprised we were back so soon, concerned that something was wrong. Jonathan turned gracious and polite, waxing enthusiastic, if briefly so, about the wonders that had been worked upon me, acting boyishly charming about how perfect everything had been, including lunch, but you know, Sir Harold, we've got a long trip back to San Francisco, and I want to get her home... Sir Harold all but winked.

Only he didn't take me home, at least not right away. He pulled into a Motel 6 maybe twenty minutes from the ranch and checked us in. He took a collar out of his pocket and put it on me. And then he fucked and buggered me until I was sore. Later, leaning on his elbow and examining my marks and bruises, he only said, "You actually have a bit of a suntan. I wouldn't have thought it possible."

He left for a little while and came back with Big Macs, fries, and big chocolate shakes, which, after the Science Diet, tasted like the best thing I'd ever eaten. We watched motel pay TV while we silently ate in bed. And then he told me to tell him about the week, and once again I made it into a long sexy story for him to jerk himself off to, which he did. And the last thing he said, before he turned off the light, was, "I'll miss your stories." I wondered, as I lay awake, listening to his even breathing, whether anyone would ever want to hear one again.

Chapter V

Entr'acte

Our last few days in San Francisco continued silent, stark, ritualistic. I don't know what would have happened if I hadn't gone to the pony farm, but I *had* gone to the pony farm, and the consequences were clear. I was out in the world now, Kate's big world. I felt I was just on loan to Jonathan in his study, and I guess so did he. What was happening between us was abstract, dreamlike. He'd do a few hours of work in the morning and then summon me, and I'd present my body to him, to use, to beat, to look at. I'd thank him afterward. I always paid attention to him, always knew what he wanted. He didn't seem moved toward any more inventiveness, and I was amazed that I had ever found his rules difficult to follow. He amused himself in the afternoons by taking me shopping, buying me pretty, expensive clothes for the trip, never asking my opinion about an item, dealing with the surprised and uncomfortable saleswomen all by himself while I didn't say anything except "Yes, Jonathan."

So the time passed and we finally took a night flight to a chilly northern European city, which I never really got a chance to see. The journey continued dreamlike, cyberspacial if you will, real time and geography squeezed into a sequence of bland, corporate interiors. We flew first class, which I'd never done before. I wanted to pig out on the champagne and quite good food, but Jonathan wouldn't let me, saying it would add to my jet lag. Rather, he made me take a Dalmane and drink a lot of water; I slept most of the way on his shoulder. A big black car with tinted windows met us at the airport and drove us straight to our hotel. We slept some more, shaking off the jet lag, and the next morning the car took us to the trials.

You didn't just get into the auction automatically. First you had to run the gauntlet of a board of examiners. My board was three men and a woman, a varied group who had seen just about everything. They had the same kind of brisk, no-nonsense attitude Kate Clarke had had and no sense of humor. Undressing in front of them, handing items of clothing to the maid who would give them to Jonathan to hold, I barely could keep from trembling, from fumbling with hooks and buttons.

The deal was that they gave you some three to five days of trials—you wouldn't know they were done until they told you. They were sitting behind a large, inlaid table in this absolutely incredible apartment in an eighteenth-century building. After the spacey, abstract-seeming twenty-four hours that had just passed, it was like leaving black-and-white Kansas for Technicolor Oz. French antique furniture, mirrors, paintings, parquet floor, where, *naturellement,* I would spend most of my time, while Jonathan sat on one of the silk-upholstered chairs, watching and smoking. I felt like a puppy again (Toto, I guess), all my earlier fantasies about being the way coolest thing they'd ever seen seeming like a million years ago. It was like the pony farm, I told myself—just pay attention, pay attention so hard that you will lose yourself in all the sensations. And I relaxed into it, realizing that I could hold back the tears only so long, concentrating on their marvelously controlled voices and careful cruelty. They found me crude and somewhat trivial, I thought, and I found myself rather adoring them.

Day one had begun with the very chic fortyish woman holding me tightly by the nipple and telling me, "We will all want to use you during these trials, but first, we will want to know how obedient you are, how much self-discipline you have. You are accustomed to being in restraints?"

"Yes, Madame Roget," I said.

They all laughed a little at this, and she told me that they didn't believe in that sort of thing for these trials. "We would not mar the woodwork of this pretty room with any of those little hooks and eyes, I think you call them. You will do everything we command, and you will be beaten, and bear it beautifully, without any collars or cuffs, without being tied or held in any way."

I gulped. "Yes, Madame Roget," I agreed, though I was terrified at the thought of not being tied down while being beaten. Too bad we couldn't rig up something using all the hardware hanging off the jacket of her Chanel suit.

Quel jour. I had no idea if I could really do it, and I wasn't perfect by any means. Twice, that I can remember, and maybe more times than that, my hands flew up to my breasts to protect them. This was at least one of the "technical" things Jonathan hadn't thought of. He, of course, loved to think of crafty ways to embed hooks and eyes all over his house and so, stupidly, hadn't realized that the rest of the world might not. I think what got me through it was that I was so pissed at him for not considering that this might happen, and so determined to best the situation in spite of him. Thanks a lot, coach, I remember thinking, seeing him out of the corner of my eye, over there on his delicate little chair. I thought of that creep who brought those terrified little four-foot-eight-inch American gymnasts to the Olympics, to be entirely outclassed by the Russians and Romanians.

That day ended very abruptly, or at least I thought so. I was on my knees in the center of the room, having just thanked the board, one by one, and very sweetly and clearly, though in a bit of a choked voice, for a brisk beating they'd just administered to my breasts and thighs. (Oh, and in French—we switched to French for the afternoons.) And, no, they didn't hold up any cards with little numbers on them to rate my performance. They hardly acknowledged me at all, in fact, but Madame Roget turned to Jonathan and curtly said, "Bring her around tomorrow at ten, and we'll continue."

"Thank you, Madame," Jonathan replied, getting to his feet and hurrying to help me up. "I will. Thank you all." He spoke like the well-brought-up little boy he must have been once. And I realized that part of the entertainment, for him, and maybe for me as well, was that he was on trial too.

When we got back to the hotel room, he grabbed me, and, very uncharacteristically, pushed me onto the bed practically into a backward somersault, pulled up my skirt, and started fucking me. My shoes went flying, and I felt a garter unsnap painfully against my thigh. Against my cunt, my belly, my legs, I felt his pants zipper and a million buttons and buckles digging into me. It was silly, clumsy, uncomfortable, but I understood. It was what I needed, too. The long, horny, ritualistic day of trials, subtleties, pain, performing, and politesse had gotten to both of us, and what we both wanted was mindless, exhausting, low-tech vanilla fucking. In and out. Bang bang bang. Friction. I closed my eyes and came a lot, moving however I pleased and making lots of noise and trying to forget that there were such things as rules or form or sensibility.

Still, you don't forget a year of slave training just like that, so a long while after, when I had recovered enough, I crawled to the foot of the bed and knelt there at attention (although I was unsure what to do about the skirt that was still up around my waist and the stockings down around my ankles). Jonathan looked at me for a while. Then he frowned, sighed, and finally said, "Oh hell, Carrie, I don't think I can maintain any rules tonight, not after watching those pros do it all day. Let's just take showers and zone out. Are you hungry? Want to do room service?"

Which was how we passed the next three evenings. We'd come back from the trials, pull off our clothes, fuck real hard, and then eat. During some break in the second day trials, Jonathan had gone out, found an English-language bookstore, and scooped up a shopping bag full of mysteries and sci fi. We weren't following rules anymore, which meant we could say anything we wanted. But we were afraid of saying wrong or embarrassing things to each other. At least I was. So the books kept us busy during those weird, wired, exhausted, polite, and oddly companionable evenings. We'd dive into them, every so often one or the other of us finishing one, maybe briefly recommending it, or tossing it across the room, proclaiming it a "turkey, guessed it halfway through, don't bother."

On the fourth evening, the rock 'n' roll/cyberpunk story I was racing through reminded me of thrash music and I thought of my Primus T-shirt, packed up with my stuff at Stuart's. I decided that if I passed the trials I'd tell Jonathan he could have it as a good-bye present. Thanks for the memories, I guess, and for the strange intimacy, even if we'd only had about four real conversations in the space of a year and a half. Good-bye, and thanks, also, for finding me a job that was not just a job but an adventure. So long, accomplice, collaborator, coconspirator.

Just then, there was a knock at the door. Jonathan went to get it. There were two European guys in suits and short squared-off haircuts, looking like the cops in *La Femme Nikita*. They were from the auction committee, though, and they were here to tell us—well, Jonathan, really—that I'd passed the trials. I could hear that much anyway, though the one of them who was doing the talking, the only one who knew English I think, was speaking very softly. I heard Jonathan tell him, "I'll fax them the papers within an hour. And I'll get her for you now."

I hadn't known they came for you in the middle of the night. And I don't know if Jonathan had either. He walked over to me—I was sprawled on the bed in a hotel bathrobe and a pair of his socks—and pulled me to my feet. "You're in," he said, "and you're not allowed to speak anymore." So much for the T-shirt idea. Or for even a so long. "Take off your clothes," he continued in an expressionless voice. "You'll go with these gentlemen."

They were standing by the door watching without much interest. I felt a little sorry for them; this had to be the dullest master/slave scene they'd barged in on. I pulled off the socks and robe, folded my glasses on top of the open book, and walked over to them. They produced a pair of high heels and a trench coat and helped me into them. Then, silently, they hustled me out of the room and shut the door behind them.

CHAPTER VI

Long Corridors

They led me down the long aseptic hotel hall—this was a hotel people stayed in for business, not pleasure—to the elevator and through the lobby. One of them—not the one who had spoken—had his hand on my arm, which he held very tightly. I was pretty scared. After all, I was in a foreign country, without money or passport, being taken god knew where by two neatly dressed thugs. Still, I had to ask myself, what was I afraid of? A white slave ring? Uh, Carrie, hate to break it to you at this late date, but that's exactly what you're in the middle of. Unless this was really some kind of bizarre Interpol spy story like one of the books I'd read. But that was even less likely. Maybe, I considered, all the sex stuff is true, but the money angle is a big scam. Now *that* was a frightening thought. And thinking of the money angle reminded me that what we really looked like—what the people in the lobby probably thought was happening if they happened to notice us at all—was two plainclothes cops with a prostitute they'd busted and were escorting out of a classy hotel.

The black car was parked on the street near the hotel, with another thug in the driver's seat. We got into the back and—dumb as it sounds I found this mildly comforting—they pushed me to the floor and had me suck their cocks. Maybe they had found the situation reasonably interesting after all, or, more likely, I thought, this was just their routine. Afterward, they joked among themselves, smoked Gauloises, and gave me a few drags. I didn't understand the language they were speaking, but they seemed to like my haircut, stroking my head, tugging at my pubic hair. I guess the joke — I mean, I don't think these guys were any too swift or subtle — was that my pubic hair was longer. They were also interested in the marks on my ass, examining them clinically. I think they saw lots of beat-up asses and just liked to keep tabs to keep a running score. After a while, it seemed like they were losing interest in me, although they still stroked and grabbed in an absent-minded way. But I think they were talking about sports or taxes or something. They seemed like pleasant enough goons, probably with wives and kids. Their ordinariness calmed me down a little.

The car stopped in front of a large, low, old, official-looking building with a semicircular driveway in front of it. I couldn't help wondering if it was some kind of a police station, because that's really what it looked like. Maybe it was a sting operation, maybe the thugs were really double agents. Maybe they were finally onto the slave thing, maybe somebody had really gotten hurt. It was, after all, pretty amazing that nobody had up until now, I thought, though in fact I had never felt like I was in that kind of danger at all.

We walked up a few low steps. It was very quiet. The building seemed to front on some sort of park, and I realized that we were no longer in the center of the city. The night was foggy and the streetlights were very bright, diffusing into a layered, pale gray glow. One of the thugs rang a buzzer, and a guy who looked like a security guard opened the door and let us into an anteroom. Marble-tiled floor, desk, a few other pieces of furniture, some dark, anonymous paintings on the wall. The thug who could speak English parked me in a corner and told me to take off the coat and shoes and give them back to him. The security guard had a small, thonged whip hanging from his belt. Nope, not the police station after all. He went to a fax machine, took out a piece of paper, compared it to the papers the thugs were shoving at him, and signed his name a lot of times. The thugs signed a few times as well, seemed satisfied, and trooped out.

The security guard, or whatever he was, came over to where I was standing and pinched and slapped me a few times. He flicked his whip idly over my breasts and poked its handle lightly at the opening of my vagina. I stayed pretty still, just trembling a little. The marble floor was cold under my feet and it was very quiet. Then he sighed, walked over to the desk, stapled all his papers together, and filed them in a folder on the desk. He picked up the desk phone, dialed an extension, spoke softly into it, and hung up. He was very young, I realized, not much more than eighteen, dark, broad-shouldered, beetle-browed, a bit stocky, just past pimply.

He sat on the edge of the desk, one leg dangling, and motioned me to come over, nodding at the floor in front of him. I knelt, watching him uncertainly. Then he took a small rubber ball out of his pocket and tossed it at the opposite corner of the room. I figured I knew what he wanted, but I waited for the light flick of his whip against my ass before I set off, on hands and knees, to fetch the ball with my mouth. When he took it back from me, he slapped my face and tossed the ball again, and I understood that I had not been fast enough. It took me about six or seven tries to get it right, and then he raised the ante. From one of the many pockets of his fatigue-type khaki pants, he took out a string of five or six small metal balls, looking like those plastic pop-bead necklaces I used to wear when I was a little girl. The balls were about the size of Ping-Pong balls. He inserted one into my asshole. Then I felt another swipe of the whip, and we continued the game. I tried to be as fast as I could and not drop the ball out of my asshole, while the rest of them flapped behind me like a crazy, horrible little tail. He seemed to enjoy this and had just graduated to pushing the second ball up me, when, thank goodness, a woman walked into the room. He quickly stood at attention, jerking me up, too, and quickly and rather painfully retrieving the string of balls as well.

The woman was tall and serious and wore a black sweater and leather pants. She smiled at the security guard, and they chatted a bit, again in a language I didn't understand. She carried a small black laptop computer and had the same whip hanging from her belt. She looked me over, went to a small dresser, and took out a collar and set of cuffs. She quickly put them on me and hooked my hands to the back of my neck. Then, nodding to the security guard, who slumped in a chair on the other side of the room, she sat down at the desk and sorted through the papers he'd put in the folder. She opened up the laptop and typed a bunch of entries into it.

She was terrific to look at. In her late twenties, maybe thirty. Very thick shoulder-length hair, a full mouth, flaring cheekbones, wide shoulders, and slim hips. She picked up the desk phone and dialed an extension. "Paul? Margot. They dropped off Lot 14 here just now. Let's do it, okay?" Her accent was distantly British, probably not English, more like Australian or South African, overlaid with a few years of California, maybe. She continued, "Yeah, fine. I think so. No,

I know you've got a file. Uh, let me see...uh, yeah, Carrie Richardson. See, you *do* have a file."

Well, you could wish to be Lot 49 in the auction, but you couldn't really insist on it, I supposed. Meanwhile, a guy who was probably Paul came in. He was thin, spiky-haired, and blond, with big glasses and lots of nervous energy. He was also wearing black, with a whip hanging from his belt, but he was wearing jeans and Dr. Martens. He carried a thick, messy, folder. All of a sudden the room seemed very busy.

"Let's have a look at her," he said. "Come here, Carrie," he called to me. I walked over and he grabbed the ring in the front of my collar. "C'mon, c'mon," he said, pulling me along and flicking his whip lightly over my calves. "Bend over the desk," he said, and I did.

They both leaned over me.

"A few marks," she said. "What do you think?"

"Needs a few more," he said. "Definitely. It'll make all the difference in the photograph. But just a few. You know how they get when we bring them merchandise that's too marked up. It's dicey—mark her up enough for the catalog, but not so much that it won't clear up before auction day itself. But we can do it. I can do it. Hey, I also have another idea. Before we actually get her up there, how about spanking her? Might be really effective, her butt all bright pink."

"It's a possibility," she said, fingering my asshole thoughtfully. "Let's see how she'd look." She sat down on the desk next to me. "Okay, Carrie," she said. "Over my knee now." I froze for a moment. It wasn't as though nobody had ever spanked me during my year at Jonathan's, but it had not been very often. I was much more used to whips, canes, and belts, and the necessary distance they put between me and the person doing the beating. Being spanked, with somebody's bare hand, lying naked across their lap, seemed much more intimate and humiliating to me. I moved toward her, finally, but she had picked up on my hesitation.

Very tentatively, I lay down over her lap. She was strong and sharply pulled me into place. And she was annoyed at me. "God, Paul," she said. "Did you catch that? Little prima donna doesn't want to get spanked. They are just so damn fussy, these little packages of merchandise. They think that because we're not buying and selling them, they don't have to obey us. We'll deal with that tomorrow, though."

Even though I didn't think I was allowed to speak, I started to apologize, but she wasn't listening. Just started spanking—hard and rhythmically. Her hands seemed enormous, covering wide swaths of me every time. She wasn't, I realized, looking for an emotional effect on me; she was interested in getting my ass a bright, even pink as quickly as possible. From my point of view it was taking a long time, and it was making me cry loudly. The crying, I couldn't help thinking, of Lot 14, and I was sure there'd be a lot more of that to come. Paul, who was watching over her shoulder, shoved a balled-up, not entirely clean, handkerchief into my mouth to gag me.

"Thanks," she said to him. "I could hardly hear myself think. How does she look?" keeping up the whacks as she spoke.

"Sure," he returned companionably, continuing to watch eagerly, "Oh good, very good, Margot. Five more strokes?"

"Seven," she said, and it was a *long* seven. My ass felt cooked. Hot, evenly hot, stewed, grilled, whatever—it was painful and tender. I imagined a cube of butter melting on it; I could almost hear the sizzle.

"Done," she said finally. "So, is this a possibility?"

Paul grabbed my shoulders and stood me up. The handkerchief was still in my mouth, and I was still sobbing and sniffling a little.

"Not bad at all," he said, remembering at last to take back his handkerchief. "Well, I think it's a go. I'll see that it gets on George's instructions, and I'll add a gag for her to his stuff. Okay?"

"Sure," she agreed. "Why not? Probably add five thou to her price right there. Okay, so much for the creative part. And I've entered her into the schedule for exercise, depilation, weighing, and measuring, all that stuff. No allergies, regular diet. And it's clear from her file that she'll do better the more fucking she gets, so I've coded her on the high end of Level II. We've got to photograph her tomorrow morning, so can you come whip her at about ten? Are you busy?"

"I'll move some things around," he said.

"Great, love," she said. "Now, what have I forgotten? Never hurts to have another pair of eyes."

He hit some keys on her computer, turned to her, and said, "Looks good. Just type in her punishment for tomorrow."

She typed something in. "It affects some of the other databases," she said, "but I think it works anyway. It's good I fixed that Level II glitch. Well," she continued, "I guess I can read her her rights and put her to bed. On your knees, Carrie, at attention at my feet."

I hurried to do it and tried to present a graceful, compliant front as I gazed at her.

"I'm sure," she began, "that it's not really necessary to point out that 'reading you your rights' is just a little joke we

146

have around here, a private name for the lecture I'm about to deliver. Because if you think you have any rights around here, somebody has made a terrible mistake. But you seem to understand what's going on. So…"

She paused for a moment and then continued. "Now," she said, "I've been calling you by name, because that's what you're used to, and it was easiest to process you in that way. But you're completely entered into our system now, and for most of our personal interactions, you won't really need a name. 'Slave' is quite adequate and a good deal more accurate. This is a warehouse, a processing center, and also a display center. We take care of all you little packages of merchandise that will be auctioned off this Friday. We take excellent care of the flesh—some of you are ridiculously expensive—we package and display you to make sure you are appealing to buyers. But we also have a more subtle responsibility—to the spirit, which demands abuse and contempt.

"For what we understand is that although most of you think of yourselves as slaves, you really have not the faintest notion of the concept. You, for example, have served one man for a year. Oh, I know you've participated in little entertainments he arranged, but they've been trivial. And you did the pony thing, which is certainly good experience, but limited. Essentially, you had a lover, a *boyfriend* (she said the word contemptuously), not a master, however he chose to superintend your activities. He organized his life around you every bit as much as he commanded you to organize yours around his. We don't consider that kind of situation an exercise of your capacity for obedience.

"Now, you'll only be here five days, but we think you'll find them instructive. You will find, in any case, that nobody here is particularly interested in you, in your little quirks of personality or individuality. We value you—all of you—as rather unique commodities that will be sold for a lot of money. Our job is to pass you through our very well-designed system. It's our system that's your master, and all of us who administer it are your masters and mistresses.

"This means Paul and I, of course, but it also means Karl over there, and all the people on our payroll—cooks, security guards, garbage men, and so forth. You will address us all as Master or Mistress, when you address us at all. We will indicate when you may speak—be careful to understand our wishes. And keep your body as open and displayed as possible. I like the way your arched back offers your breasts to me, but your legs are too close together, your pubis too hidden. That's better. Now keep your chin up, but lower your eyes. You're not allowed to look us in the face. If it helps you to discipline your gaze, remember to concentrate on the whip we all carry at our belts. When possible, your hands will be bound, but when they are not, you must remember not to touch yourself. That's all. We'll take care of you completely during your brief stay here. You'll hear the details as you need to hear them. Well, what do you say, slave?"

"Yes, Mistress," I managed. "Thank you, Mistress."

She rose. "I'm giving you back to your Master Karl now. He'll get you to bed. And Paul and I will see you tomorrow for your whipping, your photograph, and your punishment."

"Thank you, Mistress," I repeated. Paul prodded my hip with one of his Dr. Martens, and I found myself saying, "Thank you, Master," in his general direction as well.

Then they left me on my knees there, looking meekly at the floor. I was tired. It had been a long day. I couldn't quite focus my understanding on everything Margot had said, but I knew that these next days would be different than anything I'd known thus far. I felt lost, really. I was frightened, and, I realized, obscurely thrilled that something really new was beginning to happen. I wanted to lose myself some more, dive into the swirling, vertiginous feeling she had created, but just then I realized that Master Karl was standing over me.

Great. An oafish teenage master. About the least attractive person who'd ever been thrown my way. I mean, I knew that was the point, but I was tired, damn it. I don't think he knew much English, but I guess he'd mastered what he needed to know.

"Lick my boots," he managed, and I muttered, "Yes, Master," and did. I could hear him moaning. He was really getting off on it, and I started to hope that his teenage boyness would get the better of him and he'd come in his pants. Because if he didn't...

He didn't. I was going to have to get behind this scene, I knew. He pulled me to my feet by the collar and bent me over the desk. I heard him unzip his fly, and I was afraid this was going to hurt terribly. Relax, I told myself, open up. You can do it...slave. I heard this last in Margot's voice. Her lecture. I started to play it over in my head. It's the system, I thought, the system is your master. He jammed his cock into my asshole, and I just kept thinking, the system, the system, the big, beautiful, well-designed system. And as Karl kept pumping away, I kept hearing Margot, and then I kept seeing her mouth, which I was glad I had gotten a look at before she told me I couldn't look at her face. I was crying really hard, but I kept seeing her, her hips in the leather pants, her hands on the computer keys. She had, I thought, designed this hideous, awful, beautiful system. She had created all this pain and humiliation for me.

Karl cried out and collapsed on top of me. I could feel him shrinking within my raw, abused asshole, and I could feel various buttons and buckles of his pseudomilitary uniform biting into my back and legs. I wept and wept, but it was partly with relief that it was over. I'd gotten through it. But no way did I feel anything but outrage at being violated by this dim-witted creep, and no way was I ever going to feel any kind of respect or sexy abasement in front of him. It had been my sexy images of Margot that had gotten me through it. Margot and her system. I guess I'd cheated. Sue me.

Karl pulled me up and then pushed me to my knees. I was glad I didn't have to look at his face to see the mulish satisfaction I knew I'd find there. He unhooked my hands so that I could put his cock back in and zip up his fly. Then he pulled me to my feet and pushed me in front of him. He opened a door and we walked down a corridor. A few doors down, he put his hand on my shoulder to stop me. Then he went into a little kitchen and came back a minute or so later with a glass of what looked like milk. It was. Warm milk, to help me sleep, I hoped, and I also hoped it was drugged. He pushed me on, through some more corridors, and we finally came to a room, all white, with a white iron bed in it. There was a ring embedded in the wall above the bed with a chain dangling from it. He nodded to the bed, and I lay down on my side. He pulled the chain through the ring in the front of the collar and loosely attached my cuffs to it as well. Then he covered me with a light blanket. I settled into a fairly comfortable position, dimly aware (the milk must have been drugged) that I was falling asleep in the same position that O did, her first night at Roissy, in the Guido Crepax illustration.

I woke up the next morning with the sun—cold, bluish northern light—streaming into the little white room. There were gauze curtains at the window, and they moved a little, as a mild, fresh breeze blew in. It took me a minute or so to remember how I got here. I stretched tentatively and realized that the chain was long enough so that I could sit on the bed or stand at its side. I felt okay, considering. Actually, I felt pretty good, except for the fact that I was hungry and had to pee rather badly. I wasn't groggy at all—if the milk had been drugged, they'd known how much was the right amount to use. I remembered that one of the papers I'd signed—it seemed very long ago—had authorized my doctor, Jonathan's doctor, to disclose just about everything to these people. I thought of Paul's thick folder. What did they know about me? Everything, perhaps. I stood up and stretched as well as I could. And the day could hold anything.

I remembered then that it would definitely hold a whipping for me. At 10:00, Margot had said. Actually, she had said a whipping and a punishment, and while I could hope she hadn't spoken clearly, that the whipping *was* the punishment, really I knew better. There was no clock in the room, so I didn't know what time it was, but from the look of the bright sunlight, I figured 10:00 wasn't that far away.

The doorknob rattled, and a slender young woman dressed as a maid, or a nurse, or maybe a nun, entered. I lowered my eyes quickly, so I didn't really get to look at her face, but I think she was pretty, sweet-faced, about my age. Her very simple, uniform-like dress and coif-like head covering were white, and she also wore a large white apron, and I could see the handle of the ever-present whip sticking out of the apron's pocket. She carried a white china chamber pot and had a towel draped over her arm. Putting the chamber pot between my legs, she pointed downward. I squatted and peed, and then she wiped me very gently with the towel, which was warm and slightly damp. Then she left, to return in a few minutes with a pan of gruel-like food, a saucer of water, and another towel. She put them on a low table in the corner of the room. Then she unchained me from the bed and attached my hands together behind me.

She gestured to the table. I figured that I was supposed to kneel down and lap the food and water, so I did. It tasted dull and nourishing, but not bad. I mean, I guess that people don't become sex slaves for the cuisine, and at least this was recognizable people food, a healthy rice cereal. If it was any indication of how I'd be eating here, I figured they'd be giving me tofu for dinner (I was right, too). After I finished, she wiped my face with the second towel.

The morning continued silently. There was a little bath-room—also all white—off my room. She removed my collar and cuffs, placed my hands at the nape of my neck, and helped me into the big, claw-footed tub, where she gently scrubbed and rinsed me, then helped me out and dried me. She cut my nails, rubbed some nice oil into my skin. She even brushed my teeth. I liked it all, this Elizabeth Arden treatment. I knew the point was to treat me like an object, hopefully an expensive one. It wasn't bad. A woman had designed this system, I thought.

After the maid had dried me off, she led me back into the bedroom, to a sunny spot by the window. She put the collar and cuffs back on, and hooked my hands behind my neck again. Then she gently pushed me down, by the shoulders, to a kneeling position. While she quickly made the bed and tidied up a little, I found myself trying to adopt the position Margot had commanded last night. The maid stroked my cheek and very softly kissed me on the forehead. Then she left the room. Her footsteps were silent, and the door barely clicked as she shut it behind her.

I stayed quite still for the next ten minutes or so, just waiting, making sure my back was arched, legs open, chin up, eyes facing downward. I tried to breathe very slowly and deeply, practicing what I had learned in yoga class. And I tried to enjoy this momentary physical well-being and not to worry about what was to come. Yeah, right. But the breathing did help. Even if I was emotionally agitated, my body and some important part of my spirit were relaxed and ready.

Finally, I heard a sound at the door, and the bright, quiet little space became very busy as Paul and Margot strode in, both still dressed in black. They sure could fill up a room. Paul carried a leather satchel and a big, professional-looking camera. Margot also had a satchel and her laptop. They parked their equipment on the little table and jerked me to my feet. Together, they commenced a brusque yet very meticulous inspection of just about every part of me, poking, prodding, shoving.

"It says in her file," Paul remarked, "that she's always got those shadows under her eyes. It's okay; I like it. I'll light the room to play it up. I'll depend on you, though," turning to Margot, "for the right expression on her face."

Margot just nodded thoughtfully. Then she turned to me.

"Slave," she said, "stand against that wall. Best posture. Hands behind your neck. Elbows wide apart. Legs slightly apart and pelvis angled forward."

While I tried to follow her instructions, feeling my breasts lift as I spread my elbows, Paul turned on some very bright lights that were mounted on the wall across from me. He fiddled with a bank of knobs and switches (they were in a little box, also mounted on the wall), adjusting the angle and brightness of the lights. I had just about gotten myself arranged in a position I thought Margot would like, when she called, "And you can raise your eyes. Look straight at me."

Paul began to shoot photographs, feeling his way through subtle variations in angles and lighting. Meanwhile, Margot carelessly said to me, "Oh yes, and I've forgotten to tell you your punishment. For slowness to obey and talking out of turn yesterday. You'll be displayed in the staff cafeteria tonight at dinner. Swing shift will have you for dessert."

Paul snapped another picture, and Margot shot me a self-satisfied look. Clever bitch. I guess my ill-concealed surprise and outrage had been what they'd wanted all along.

"That's it," he called, jubilantly. "Super, Margot. On the bed, slave, hands and knees." And Margot added, "And no more looking us in the face."

I hurried onto the bed, while he got a set of straps out of his satchel. Very quickly and expertly, he trussed my wrists to my ankles, so that my ass was correctly angled at him. A few more straps, and I was immobile on the bed. He had brought a real gag this time, thick padded material, that tied at the back of my head. Then he took out a last strap, doubled it, went into the bathroom, and held it under the water for a while, stiffening the leather. Then he dried off the excess water and started his meticulously placed, hard strokes. It hurt more than Jonathan's cane. I wept, choked, and gurgled behind the gag. Thank god I couldn't move. There weren't that many strokes, however, though I could feel when they crisscrossed each other, no doubt the dark welts creating a most impressive cross-hatching effect. At least, Margot thought so, helping unstrap me and affectionately telling Paul, "You do good work."

They could see that I was pretty teary-eyed and knocked out by the whipping, so they just dragged me to the wall and attached my wrist cuffs over my head to the chain I'd been attached to the previous night. Working very quickly and well together, they got the bed out of the way, readjusted the lights, and prodded me into the right position. This was an easy one for Paul, I guess, since he didn't have to worry about my facial expression in this rearview shot. He even kept the gag on, partly, I think, so they wouldn't have to listen to me, but certainly for documentary effect as well. It all went very quickly. Then he ungagged me, packed all his equipment, and hurried out, leaving me with Margot.

She unchained me and freed my hands. "Kneel up at my feet," she told me, and I did, while she typed some more into her computer. I kept my eyes focused on her hands. Finally she closed the cover. Her hands were folded in her lap and I could feel her eyes on me.

"We take care of you slaves in several ways here," she began. "First of all, we prepare for the auction by getting all your information together for the big, glossy catalog we produce for potential buyers. That's why you're here for five days; that's how long it takes us to put it together and get it printed up. We've got your photographs now and they'll

weigh and measure you at the gym later, and that's about it —
I think we know just about everything we need to know
about you.

"And of course we feed you and keep you clean, rested,
exercised, and fucked. I'm sure I don't have to tell you that
anybody who comes to your room to fuck you is your master
or mistress, to be obeyed completely. And of course you'll
obey the trainers in our gym just as completely. You'll be
working out for two and a half hours every day. It's really
pretty businesslike, and slaves don't usually disobey the
trainers, probably any more than Cher or Madonna does. See
that you're good, though, because of course you could be
punished if you don't cooperate fully.

"Other than that, though, this is a display center. Buyers
come here to check you out. They can schedule visits to your
room, but mostly they do their shopping in the Garden.
Which is where you're going next. You don't really need to
know more than that. Actually, you don't really need to know
that, and I'll be explaining why in a minute. Well, what do
you say to me?"

I murmured my appreciation, not forgetting to address
her as "Mistress," and she continued. "Now, let's talk about
punishment. We are constrained, of course, in our choice of
punishments because we want you to be relatively unmarked
when you're sent to the auction. So exposure and humiliation
are what we use."

She reached into her satchel, and pulled out two neatly
lettered, laminated cardboard placards. They each said
SLOW TO OBEY/TALKED OUT OF TURN, and she attached one
in front and the other in back, so they dangled from the
rings in my collar. "You'll wear these inside our staff areas

156

all day," she said, "so that any staff member who happens to see you will know that you're to be among the slaves displayed this evening. It's up to them how they use you. Sometimes they squabble over the slaves they want the most, and sometimes they design group games. It's a good punishment, but it makes life difficult for me, because I have to modify your routine online. And since every time a buyer wants extra time with you there's a systemwide ripple effect—fuzzy logic and all—the extra modifications are no fun. So don't make me have to punish you again." She slapped me on the cheek.

"No, Mistress," I said clearly. "I won't, Mistress."

And then she reached into her satchel and took out a small bracelet, which she buckled snugly onto my left wrist. It was made of soft leather, and I could feel wires embedded in its underside. She opened her laptop and pressed a key, and I felt a small set of prickles from the bracelet's wires, as though the points of many tiny pins were being stuck into the inside of my wrist. I guessed it was a buzz from the wires, the mildest possible electric shock, but somehow encoded to feel sharp, metallic rather than electrical.

"This will alert you to get to your next station," she said. "No, you won't know where it is. You'll have to consult one of the Arguses," and she led me to a small computer screen mounted in the wall of my room, near the door.

"You wave this stud on the bracelet over the little light," she said, holding my wrist and doing it for me. I heard that crabby little computer disk reading sound, somewhere between a click and a postnasal drip, and the screen lit up, showing me a schematic map of myself and my surroundings, with arrows pointing me where to go next. It was actually pretty clear, at least in direction, though I didn't know where I'd be when I got there.

"We have lots of these," she said, "two hundred and fifty-six of them, actually. So you can't get too lost, and of course we can always find you. But the signal at your wrist will become a little stronger in five minutes, so you'll want to hurry. When you get to where you're going, you can log in at the Argus, and then the signal will stop. Until, of course, it's time for you to move on."

"Well," she said, "I think you'd better go. But what do you say, slave?"

The bracelet's prickles got just a little sharper as I thanked her again, as though slightly bigger needles were going just slightly farther into my flesh. I waved it over the Argus again, to review the directions, and then I hurried in the direction the screen described to me. I was going down a long corridor, past purposeful people, some naked, some clothed, everybody, it seemed, going somewhere fast. Some of the people with clothes on looked appreciatively at the signs hanging from my collar. As I hurried to the Garden, I tried not to think of what that would mean for me that evening.

The diagram on the Argus screen had been pretty schematic, but quite adequate and accurate. Out of my little room, quite a ways to the left down a long corridor, a little way more to the right, through a door, and then into a large open space, maybe halfway into the center. Just before I got to the door of the large open space, the pinpricks from my bracelet got a notch sharper. This time it was really painful, but I almost didn't notice, I was so amazed to see what there was through the large open door.

It was astonishing. A huge, beautiful, domed area, maybe twice as big, I guessed, as one of those big domed baseball stadiums. Fountains, large potted trees, beautifully raked gravel paths and many, many flowers. It didn't pretend to be outdoors; there wasn't Astroturf or anything on the ground—mostly beautifully colored tiles and gravel, ivy and some hardy succulents growing in shallow beds. But there was a lot of green, considering, and running water, streams and little waterfalls, and small hills and winding paths through miniature arbors. The dome was made of sinuous art deco ironwork, like the boulevard Saint-Michel Metro station, and through its huge glass panels you could see that cold blue-gray northern winter sky, contrasting with the balmy temperature within. This was the Garden, I guessed, but I had to think of it as a pleasure dome, decorated with fairy lights and the naked and sometimes adorned bodies of the slaves scattered throughout it.

A security guard was standing at the door looking bored. "Log in at the Argus," he said, and after I did, he took the signs off my collar. "You don't wear these for the rich people," he said, "but you're in trouble if you don't get them back from me after you do your thing in there. And hurry up," he said, shoving me through the door.

If he hadn't, I probably would have just stood there gaping, ignoring the pain in my wrist until it jumped another notch, but I hurried to the next Argus, embedded in a low wall next to a small café on a brick terrace. I almost bumped into a bearded man in a pale gray suit, blissfully leaning against the wall, while a naked red-haired boy sucked him off. I buzzed myself in, and the prickles in my wrist stopped. I was finally where I needed to be, I guessed, as I stood there taking in the scene some more. At the tables, drinking wine and coffee and eating ices, were a few very elegant people, dressed in soft silks and linens, as though they were visiting a resort in the middle of winter. More of them strolled down the paths, talking, laughing, and pointing out the sights, the slaves posed as living statuary on pedestals, columns, and fountains, or beautifully masked as animals in cages in the little zoo or on the tiny carousel by the lake. Every so often, if a slave seemed inviting enough, one of the sightseers would simply gesture to him or her and the slave would approach and strike a position, offering mouth, ass, cock, or cunt — rather like the presentation competitions Jonathan had, once upon a time, taken me to. It was a lot to take in — the bigness and the prettiness of the space, the well-bred tinkling laughter that seemed to be everywhere, the absolute graceful obedience of all the slaves, and my own stupid, naked amazement in the middle of it.

Just then a man dressed as a waiter thrust a tray of refreshments at me. "The table by the lemon tree," he said, and I hurried over. I was a part of it now and I was determined to do it right. Don't spill a drop, I told myself. Stand straight and never mind that they are clothed and powerful and you are naked and totally at their mercy. And if you can feel your breasts bounce a little, and you can feel their eyes upon you...well, just don't spill a drop of these refreshments you are carrying to these frightening people in this beautiful, demonic place. I was at the table now.

"The ices?" I asked politely, holding up the delicate goblet. A pretty young woman with short black curls and pink-and-white porcelain skin smiled and nodded. So far so good. "Beer?" I continued. Same with the thickset older man with the graying hair and beard. The tea went to the tall, angular man with the shaved head. I put it down in front of him and was preparing to nod politely and withdraw when he reached a large hand behind me and grabbed a big chunk of my ass. Which was quite painful, as you can imagine, given the beating less than an hour ago. I tried not to show it.

"I like it," the bald man said, "when I can get a lot of an ass into my hand. And I like the feel of this one. Welts, too. Perhaps she's been naughty, or more likely somebody just thought she'd be more provocative this way. What do you think, Francis, Chloe?" And to me he said roughly, "Turn around for the lady and gentleman, you."

I held the tray in front of me and slowly turned my back to the table. "Bend over," the bald man said, moving his heavy hand to the small of my back and pressing. I bowed at the waist, keeping my back straight, letting them have a good look at Paul's handiwork. I felt like a baboon, presenting my decorated ass to them, and tried to console myself by bowing as gracefully as I could, stretching my hamstring muscles as though I were at ballet class. I felt grateful that I didn't have to look these people.

Francis, the bearded man, sounded a bit bored. "Is it necessary, André," he asked, "to encourage Chloe this way?" And to Chloe, he asked, "Well, are you satisfied, now that you're here?"

She spoke softly, but very clearly, and I could tell that she didn't need the least encouragement. "Yes, Francis," she said, "it's as interesting as I expected. And I don't think she's been a naughty girl. I think André is right and somebody thought she'd be improved by those marks. Send her over to me, André."

161

"Call her yourself," he returned shortly.

"You," she said, "slave, put down that tray and come over here immediately and face me."

I walked over, my eyes down. She spanked my breasts a little with the cold bottom of her spoon. "Too small for you, Francis," she said. "I suppose André and I are just wasting your time with this one."

He nodded, and in fact he was looking across the field, some bigger ones having doubtless caught his eye. "Why don't I meet you two in a hour?" he said. "I'll tell that waiter up there to turn her little bracelet off for a while."

Thanks, Francis, I thought, as he hurried off. André took a leash out of his pocket and handed it to Chloe, and she attached it to my collar. "What would you think," she said, "a little jeweled collar, painted toenails, nipples gilded to match? Maybe powder blue, hmmm? And a pretty little kennel for her to crawl into. It's sweet, isn't it, that little bit of sadness about her."

"But it's too bad," she continued, "that we're not allowed to make her even sadder. Why can't we whip her, or at least watch somebody do it?"

"Be logical," he answered, "with the crowd that's out to buy this week, she'd be hamburger by the time of the auction. But it's still fun, isn't it, to see her working to control her humiliation. I always enjoy that part."

And I was blushing rather furiously. I think it was the painted toenails, the idea of being her pet in a jeweled collar. She pushed me to my knees. "Now follow me on all fours," she said. "André," she added, "are you really going to walk behind us in that ridiculous way?"

"Just, you know, to make sure she holds herself well," he mumbled, his eyes, no doubt, on my welted ass.

The tiled walkway was hard, cold, and smooth under my knees and the palms of my hands. She led me around the little artificial lake, stopping once or twice to talk to friends or acquaintances who also had slaves in tow. Finally she sat down on a bench by the lake, where it was fed by a little waterfall. "Drink," she said, and I lapped some water.

"And now eat," she said, raising her skirt, showing me a dazzling white shaved cunt, surrounded by intricate black garters and stockings. I entered her with my tongue, while she kept a tight hand on my leash. I heard her groan softly, as I licked all around, returning often to her clitoris, but circling and teasing as well.

And I wasn't entirely surprised to feel André entering my asshole, his big hands on my breasts. I tried to cry out, but Chloe kept my head buried in her. So I just gave in to their rhythms, his pushing and her pulling, and me trying to be as active and passive as it all demanded, until finally they both came and leaned over me to kiss each other hungrily.

"We'll try a boy next," he murmured to her sleepily, "a very pretty little one." Since she'd unsnapped my collar, I guessed I was dismissed.

As I scrambled to my feet, I noticed a man alone on a bench halfway around the little lake. He was looking through some papers, which seemed like an odd thing to be doing in the Garden, but it still seemed to me that he'd been watching me with André and Chloe. I don't know how I knew that, or what exactly I had even sensed, besides a vector of attention and a quality of stillness. I turned and looked at him for a moment, though all I could really catch was the glint of dark-tinted glasses. And then I remembered to lower my eyes, and I felt a pinprick at my wrist. Fuzzy logic kicking in again, I thought, as I hurried to the Argus.

The screen directed me back to my room, where a maid cleaned me up and gave me some lunch. Then I napped for an hour or so, before my bracelet led me to the gym. My punishment signs were dangling from my collar again. I waved my bracelet at the Argus, and a nearby printer started spitting out paper with information about me, so that the trainer who took charge of me knew what program to set me on, how many minutes of stretches, StairMaster, free weights.

Margot was right; it was all very businesslike. Just like a downtown yuppie gym, except that nobody was using a Walkman—they piped in some dreary upbeat Europop instead. And, of course, not to forget that everybody using the machines or the weights or the mats was a naked slave, cuffed, collared, and coded into the system. A few, like me, wore little placards announcing that they were scheduled for punishment that evening and telling anybody who was interested the nature of the transgression. Mine were pretty typical, though I also saw UNDISCIPLINED GAZE and, most provocatively, WILLFULLY DISOBEDIENT. This last one fascinated me. It hung from the collar of a tall boy using a Nautilus machine. He had very strong, beautiful thighs, the kind where there are muscles peeking out from under the muscles you can see. His long black hair was bound at the neck. I wondered what you had to do to merit WILLFULLY DISOBEDIENT, instead of just DISOBEDIENT, or my own wimpy SLOW TO OBEY/TALKED OUT OF TURN. If you'd gotten this far, why would you purposely disobey, and what exactly had tipped the balance to WILLFUL? I wondered if I'd ever find out. Well, you need something to occupy your mind when you're on the StairMaster.

You were actually still supposed to keep your gaze down, but it was hard to stick to that, and the trainers wisely didn't make a big thing about it. Mostly, you were here to work—no pain, no gain, though of course all of us already knew that. How you dealt with your feelings of arousal or humiliation or whatever this all made you feel was your own problem. I suppose everybody, like me, was covertly eyeing the competition. The slaves, or the ones I could easily peek at, ranged from okay to drop-dead gorgeous. And everybody, sweating and straining at their machines or with their weights, had, as you'd probably expect, quite a good body, or even better than that. I could only hope that whatever "quality" Kate Clarke had discerned in me would be evident to some buyer as well. Otherwise, I'd have to think about graduate school again.

Meanwhile, my eyes kept straying to Willful, who was now walking a treadmill across from me. I wanted to stare and stare at him, at the sensitive little muscles in his belly and at the root of his purplish cock, surrounded by wonderful little black curls. I guess I did stare and stare at him, though I kept trying, as Margot put it, to "discipline my gaze." I was glad when they moved me to a slant board and I had to concentrate on my own stomach muscles.

The Europop kept tinkling on, but my inner ear turned it into a cut from the oldies stations, one I hadn't even remembered I knew (one, in fact, that my mother used to annoy me with by loudly singing along whenever it came on the car radio). I sighed and reset the slant board a notch steeper. Great, Carrie, let's regress to Sexual Fantasy Number One in your whole life (and maybe it isn't really even your fantasy, maybe it's Mom's)—the Bad Boy in the Class. He's a rebel. Watch the way he shuffles his feet.

He had stepped off the treadmill, and was, in fact, just standing around shuffling his feet while the Argus, for some reason, hung. It came up, though—way to go, Margot—and he scanned his instructions. What was particularly remarkable about this place was how everybody seemed to have his or her own distinct schedule. I mean, if I'd had to handle a group of slaves, I would have treated them like a group, like in the army or elementary school or Sir Harold's place. But they didn't do that here; rather, they treated you, as Margot had put it, like a "rather unique commodity." Our paths crossed, but we didn't march in lockstep. This was, I knew, the point of Margot's complicated software. They didn't have to use regimentation here—except, I supposed, when they wanted to, when it would serve some distinctly humiliating purpose. It made me think about just how unsubtle some forms of control were and wonder what other forms of control were available, for those of us who get off on contemplating and enacting the rituals of power and domination. Jonathan had said that the idea, often as not, was to mimic the social structure of late feudalism, the *ancien régime* just at the cusp of the advent of bourgeois democracy. I was wondering just how necessary that all was, or how relevant to the strange times we were living in now, when all of a sudden Willful caught my eye, and—swear to god—quickly mouthed the words, "See you tonight." Then he sauntered out the gym door.

I was scared. I thought of Cathy and the little piece of hose. And I was sure somebody—trainer or guard—had noticed, that any minute they'd drag me off to some dark dungeon for some drawing and quartering, or maybe the rack, something tasty out of early—never mind late—feudalism. But nothing happened. If anybody had noticed, he didn't say anything. The boy, I had to admit, had timing. Street smarts, maybe. I imagined him dressed (like early Marlon Brando—Mom again) to match the song—blue jeans and a tight white T-shirt, a pack of cigarettes under his rolled up sleeve. Black Garrison belt. Engineer's boots. I found the image very hot. Well, I'd already seen him naked. And I would see him tonight, I realized.

I spent the rest of my gym time in a confused haze, the remainder of the two and a half hours floating by without my much noticing. Then my bracelet prickled and I followed the schematic back to my room, where another maid cleaned me up and gave me lots of water to drink. As usual, she left me kneeling, in the preferred position of abject attention, waiting, I supposed, for somebody to come to the room to fuck me, as Margot had promised. Cleaned, fed, rested, exercised, and fucked, she'd said. And sure enough some staff member, a really ordinary middle-level bureaucrat, I thought from the look of his shoes, came along. And fucked me silly, though I hardly got to see his face. After he left, I just lay facedown on the bed for about twenty minutes, wondering just how much of this they thought I "needed." It was an interesting question, and not an entirely unpleasant one, a whole lot more pleasant than the punishment that I was trying not to think about, as the sky darkened outside my window.

But time inched on, a maid coming by in a while to clean me up again and bring me my predicted tofu and vegetables for dinner. Then some more waiting. Yoga breathing. I hated the suspense. Finally, another security guard, not Karl, thank goodness, came in and attached some truly painful clips to my nipples, with horrid little bells attached to them, and then disappeared silently.

About fifteen minutes later, my bracelet prickled, and I followed its directions through the corridors, the little bells jingling spitefully and painfully with every step I took. I wound up at a small employee cafeteria, and a security guard at the door led me in. It was a typical, brightly lit, steam-table kind of eating place, with wood-grained Formica-topped tables and molded plastic chairs. The only thing out of the ordinary was a platform about three feet high and maybe twenty-five feet wide against one wall. Two or three slaves were already kneeling here, on hands and knees, asses against the wall, placards dangling from their collars, eyes cast down. Some of the folks eating at the tables were looking them over, pointing, joking and, I suppose, planning the good times to come — the rest were just eating, drinking coffee, hanging out, smoking, and chatting.

The guard led me to the platform, and I noticed for the first time that there was another nasty wrinkle to the system. They didn't chain you down or anything. What you did was climb onto the platform and back up — until your asshole was impaled on the dildo mounted on the wall. Thoughtfully, the dildos were mounted at different heights; the guard seemed to have a sense of which was my height — well, I guess they'd get good pretty fast at figuring that one out. It was big — big, cold, smooth, and hard — and, mercifully, well greased. I winced as I backed onto it and was rewarded by a few hoots and giggles, as well as one or two promises that I'd be accommodating a lot more than that before the evening was over. Somebody tossed a little wad of paper at me, which hit my face, then, a banana peel, which kind of bounced off my shoulder. I could feel myself blush, and I bowed my head, but the guard raised my chin with the handle of his whip. The little bells hanging from my aching breasts jingled as I arched my back to help me assume the correct position. I looked at the faces at the tables, banal, jocular, cheerful, and I really did feel punished. Abased. This was different from anything I'd experienced before. I remembered Jonathan's little speech a million years ago, the one about my jagged little edge of critical intelligence—oh please, gimme a break! These people could care less about my critical edge, about the subtleties of my consciousness, the fine balance between objectification and narrative subjectivity. I felt bereft. I didn't like to look. I had to keep my head up, but as much as I could, I lowered my eyelids. I could see those damned little bells, shiny under the fluorescent lights and slightly blurred, beneath my SLOW TO OBEY/TALKED OUT OF TURN placard. I put everything I had into trying not to cry.

A few more slaves were led in, I could see out of the corner of my eye. But I didn't need to see it when Willfully Disobedient made his entrance—I could tell he was here by the excited murmur in the crowd, the jokes and catcalls, and the little missiles that started flying at him even before he got to the platform. He was the Main Event tonight, baked Alaska or cherries jubilee for dessert, no doubt about that. I forgot about my fears a little and raised my eyelids to watch.

They got him backed up on the stage and impaled, the security guard taking advantage of his own fifteen minutes of fame by slapping him hard in the face a few times and pulling and twisting at the bells on his nipples (I noticed suddenly that there was also one hanging from his scrotum). The crowd seemed to like the guard's little show just fine, except that they would have liked to see the boy exhibit less self-control. (Secretly, frighteningly, so would I have, I realized.) Still, even I'd been able to control myself thus far, so I guess they weren't surprised that he'd done so as well. The evening was young yet.

But they were already starting to quarrel among themselves. I mean, it was obvious to me, as well as to them of course, that not all fifty people in the room were going to get a crack at the Main Event that evening. Some of them were going to have to be satisfied with the rest of us. I didn't know whether this was good or bad news for me.

In retrospect, I'm impressed at how well they worked it out—how cheerfully, fairly, and quickly. Of course, this was one of those countries where everybody gets more than a month of paid vacation every year and cradle-to-grave medical care, and they can't change computer monitors without the union's okay about the long-term health implications. Add to it an employee benefit like the one I was participating in—like the one I *was*—and why shouldn't they be decent and humane? To each other, that was.

So, as far as I could follow, the rules they improvised were: Willfully Disobedient would be fucked by two teams of ten (it would have to be men, obviously, and I could see that the women were not pleased by this, but biology *is* destiny sometimes, even under social democracy). They'd line up on either end of him, and the idea was to compete for which team took the longest to get finished coming in him. Bets were taken, though I couldn't figure out what the prizes would be.

They hustled us off the platform and dragged it to the center of the room so that everybody could see. The asshole team grabbed a big tin of some kind of EuroCrisco that somebody had brought out from the kitchen.

The rest of us were really just bit players. They attached leashes to the rings in our collars so that they could drag us on hands and knees around the crowd (they positioned us at different points). We were popcorn at the movies, mostly, for those watching the entertainment. I was vastly relieved and, somewhere deep inside, just a little insulted. Go figure.

Anyway, I was pushed down to the linoleum floor and my leash given to a hefty woman sitting near the platform. She raised her skirt and pushed my head into her crotch, where I began to lick and suck, feeling the trembling of her big belly and thighs, and hearing the shouts and laughs from the crowd.

After a while, she jerked the leash and slapped my ass, hard, and I crawled away from her, to the next hand, this one a man, who turned me around and got down behind me to fuck me up the ass. I was glad, at least, that this allowed me to see what was happening up on the platform. About what you'd expect, I guess. Willful was on his hands and knees sucking some big guy's cock, while the guy, who was dressed like a cook, grasped his pony tail to control the movement of his head. It was hard for me to see, but I had the idea that Willful wasn't just a passive mouth being manipulated, but was actually putting some action behind it. Meanwhile, the guy at his asshole side, maybe an electrician or something, had just come, to cheers from the audience, and was staggering away, while his replacement began cheerily drilling away, occasioning more cheers and calls of encouragement.

171

This seemed to encourage the guy drilling into me. I heard myself calling out in pain and was rewarded by some hard slaps against my breasts. Finally, though, he was done, pulling himself back into his seat and handing my leash to the next person, who hauled me over her knee and started spanking me (the crowd had started up rhythmic clapping, to accompany the next mouth guy's orgasm). And so it went, my simply following the jerks at the leash, relaxing into it as hands pushed or lifted me where they wanted me to go, breathing as well as I could, trying to stay as open as I could wherever I could. My knees were aching from crawling around the sticky floor, my face was sticky with come and tears, and the rest of me was a sticky, sweaty mess as well.

I was under another woman's skirts when the contest was finally over, and a huge cheer rose from the crowd, accompanied by groans and boos, I guess from those who'd bet on the losers. So I didn't get to see who won. Not that I cared. The woman grasped my head firmly, signaling that I was to finish what I was doing, and I did, until I heard her moans, and she dropped her hands entirely. A security guard picked up my leash and pulled me to my feet. I got to see Willful being pulled to his feet as well; I guess he'd fallen flat on the stage from exhaustion. The crowd shouted their disapproval at this, and then laughed as they saw how weak he was in the knees. Two big men lifted him to his feet, and then they hustled him around the cafeteria so everybody could at least get a pinch or poke at him. But he wasn't crying. He seemed, from what I could see, interested in what was happening, bleary-eyed and mostly exhausted, but still amazingly alert.

At last, the party was breaking up. As a security guard grabbed my shoulders and turned me toward the exit door, I noticed the man in the dark glasses again, standing against a wall with his arms folded, watching everything, it seemed like. At least it seemed like he was watching me. Maybe he's head of security or something, I thought idly, as I prepared to make my way down the corridors and back to my room. Leaving the cafeteria, I could hear a few shouts and guffaws behind me—I guessed they were still tormenting that tall, beautiful boy. And I never did find out what you had to do to be counted as WILLFULLY DISOBEDIENT in that place.

The next few days were much calmer. I spent a lot of time in the Garden—I was a lion in the zoo, a marvelously decorated peacock on the little carousel, a statue on the fountain, and a café waitress a few times more—and I got very quick at responding to the peremptory nod, the snap of the fingers, the contemptuous "you, there." Drop everything, climb gracefully down, pay strict attention, and open and give yourself totally to the probing fingers, the hard cocks, the slaps and pinches, the appraising comments made to companions and other buyers.

It was a bit easier in my room, waiting for whoever turned up. Sometimes they'd be buyers, sometimes staff members. The staff members just wanted to fuck me, of course. And because they couldn't mark up my skin before the auction (and my ass was healing, mercifully), there was a limit to how much they could hurt me. There were lots of slaps and spanks, lots of swipes with their whips, nothing that hurt too terribly much—it was a whip more for effect than for really doing much damage. And when the buyers came to my room, they didn't act that differently. Maybe, I thought, it was because the little white room with its iron bed seemed partly like a room in a brothel, partly like a room in a convent. It was its own ironic little turn-on. People just wanted to get fucked there.

Meanwhile, time passed in a comforting, monotonous way, a continuous present. I never saw a clock, never knew what time it was. All I knew was where I had to be and what I had to do now. I had to work hard to keep track in my head of the days to the auction; part of me felt as though I'd be here forever. Still, I tried awfully hard to obey, to assume positions well, to relax into whatever I was pushed or dragged to do. Margot's line, "the system is your master," had a resonance for me. I did think about her, though, and wonder if I'd see her again.

Then, in late afternoon of the fifth day, the night before the auction, they threw me a real curve. My bracelet led me back from the gym to my room, and there, on the bed, was a dress. It was mine, a gray-green wool, just a long, soft, sinuous button-down cardigan really, one of the pretty dresses Jonathan had bought for me to wear to visit the board of examiners—or, at least, to wear in between the hotel and their apartment. My shoes were there too, at the side of the bed. And there were stockings and a garter belt, and pretty, Victoria's Secret underwear. Silk tap pants—sexy wonderful little abbreviated boxer shorts—and little lace underwire bra that hooked in the front. All in a deep, smoky gray. I'd never worn anything like that in my life—my pre-Jonathan underwear had been standard cotton three-to-a-pack, with the occasional splurge if Jockey for Women was on sale (and of course with Jonathan I hadn't worn any at all). They'd even given me back my wristwatch. Were they throwing me out? As far as I knew, I hadn't done anything wrong.

I was really panicky. I went to the bed, and there was an unsigned note:

Take off your collar. Then shower, dress, and put on makeup. The Argus will tell you where to go.

I'd never taken off a collar. My hands trembled as I did. So easy, just buckles. They must be throwing me out. I went to the little bathroom and took a long shower, doing all the things for myself that normal people do. It felt as though I was doing it through a haze of memory. I felt quite clumsy with the makeup, but I looked good, I thought, when I'd finally finished putting it on. I felt numb, confused, cheated. I had tried so hard for so long. What had they wanted from me that I hadn't given them? It must have been the little exchange of glances with Willfully Disobedient, I was thinking, wandering around the room distractedly, waiting for the bracelet to buzz me.

When it did, I hurried to the Argus, got my diagram, and set off. This time I had to negotiate a fairly complicated set of twists and turns down corridors. I even got lost once and had to consult another Argus. But Margot had been right—you couldn't get too lost in that place. The final lap of the instructions took me up a stairway, cleverly represented on the diagram. I was beginning to feel like I was playing one of those early computer games like Adventure. I might have even enjoyed it, if I hadn't been so panicky about being thrown out.

The last corridor seemed to be offices, with some technical and educational information posted on a bulletin board. A very pretty woman in jeans and a sweatshirt that had ORACLE printed on it looked at me curiously, as I clicked by in my high heels. This, I thought, must be the place, and I headed for the Argus midway down the hall, next to the open office door.

I waved my bracelet over it and wasn't at all surprised when I heard Margot's voice from the office. I was both thrilled and terrified. "Come in," she said brusquely, and when I did she barely looked up from her screen. "I'll be just a minute," she said in a distant, distracted voice. "Sit down."

Typical, I thought, I always go for the compulsive ones. And scared as I was, I couldn't help feeling a little pissed and neglected. I sat on a wooden chair and looked around the monastic little office. A few different kinds of computers, a printer, and some other machines I didn't recognize. Neat piles of papers and printouts, scientific reprints, and many, many technical manuals. Just a few other books—Foucault, Fourier, the volume of the Sade collection that contained *Justine* and *Philosophy in the Bedroom*. In a little alcove off the office, there was a beat-up leather couch with an afghan neatly folded over the arm. There were no curtains on the window, and I could see the soft black night, a few stars, the distant lights of the city.

She breathed out a triumphant "Yesss," hit a key that started an intricate geometric screen-saver program, and turned to look at me over her shoulder, draping her arm over the back of her chair. I forgot how frightened I was and how pissed. She was wearing her leather pants, with a black silk shirt and big silver hoop earrings. And she was grinning, wickedly and delightedly, at me, at my absolute confusion, discomfort, and wild mute desire for her.

"I do like the dress," she said. "That boyfriend of yours has lovely taste. But," she continued, getting up and coming over to me, "you really don't need that bracelet." She unbuckled it and kissed the inside of my wrist. The ripple of sensation was considerably stronger than any of the electric shocks had been. But they must be throwing me out, I thought. No collar, no bracelet...

She laughed.

"Don't worry," she said. "We're not throwing you out. You don't need the bracelet because, after all, you're here with me. And I can put you back on the floor, naked and on your knees, in a minute if that's what you want. But standard procedure around here is that you get a last supper, and we treat you like a free agent for the last time, if you think you can stand it. It's your last chance to change your mind. Hey, cheer up. No tofu for dinner tonight."

A maid came to the door, pushing one of those room service tables on wheels. There was a white tablecloth on it and dinner on top of that, with big dome-like covers over the plates. I stayed in my seat, and the maid pushed the table in front of me. Margot pulled her desk chair across from me.

The table was set for two. The maid uncovered the plates. It was true. No tofu. Instead, things I loved. Pâté, to start with. And then salmon. Braised leeks. Shiitake mushrooms. Very, very good, crusty bread. It was the kind of dinner I'd imagined Jonathan buying for his girlfriends. Margot opened a bottle of wine.

"I'm not surprised you know what I like to eat," I said, digging in. I was still quite confused, but the food was putting out its own clear signals. "But everybody can't be coming here for dinner tonight."

"Everybody else is having special dinners in their rooms," she said, "but I'm so busy getting everything together for tomorrow that I pulled you up here instead. Don't worry. We have a big staff to take care of all you guys. I just over-rode the parameters and entered myself into this slot. Somebody had to do it, anyhow."

I sipped my wine, feeling very shy, suddenly. It was as though we were on some big date. She leaned over and kissed me softly on the forehead, and I could see her breast through the open collar of her silk shirt. She really was very beautiful, though you didn't see it all at once. You saw her energy, her astonishing control, a flare of collarbone, the shadow of a cheekbone. And always, I thought again, her blunt, powerful, eloquent hands.

I felt a stab of feeling in my cunt, clashing rather confusedly with my absurd joy at the lovely food. My mouth dropped open, but then I closed it and continued to chew. I was so confused that I didn't know what to feel. She had said they were treating me like a free agent. I guessed, in any case, that that meant I could say anything I wanted to say and not have to worry about them taking away my dessert. But what did I want to say? "Do you come here often?" was about the only thing that occurred to me.

"When do I have to say whether I'm changing my mind?" I asked. "I mean, I don't intend to, but if I say that right away do I have to take my clothes off immediately?"

"Basically," she said, "we get to have a nice dinner together, and then I ask you the question. You say no, you haven't changed your mind, and I make you say it in some formal way that's too corny to repeat right now. Then I call the maid and settle back to watch her take all the clothes off you and put you back into restraints and like that. It's supposed to be your final big humiliation in this place, but frankly, I'm not very impressed with it. It's left over from before I was organizing things around here. In a while, I hope to replace it with something a whole lot better. Okay? Do you think you can relax now?"

"Yes," I said, "I think so. This is a major mindfuck. But I guess I'm glad about it. This food is wonderful, and I'm glad you're here. God, that sounds terrible, I'm sorry, I didn't intend it to come out in that order, you know what I really mean. Well, anyhow, if I were really a free agent, I'd ask you how you got here. I mean, you know how I got here."

She laughed. I loved her mouth. "I understand," she said. "All that healthy bland food we've been giving you is one of our undercover humiliations. And I got here," she continued, "pretty much the same way you did. Originally, I mean. I was sold at the auction and spent a year as a slave. But the truth is I wasn't really that good at it. It was no disgrace, in fact it was pretty hot, and I have good memories of it. But I knew that I wasn't going to continue along those lines, and I had no idea what I wanted to do next. About three weeks before my term of service was due to end, my master called me into a little office he had. I'd never been there. It was a messy little room, filled with computers and assorted computer hardware, machines with their casings off and their innards hanging out. I'd never seen anything like it, and my eyes kept straying to all the boards and cable. I was on my knees in front of him, and all of a sudden he slapped me so hard he knocked me over.

"'You're not paying attention, Margot,' he said. 'You're going to get a very serious whipping tonight.'

"'Yes, sir,' I said unhappily. 'Thank you for correcting me, sir.'

"'But meanwhile,' he said, 'I'm going to leave you alone in here for the afternoon. There are hardware and software manuals on the shelf. See how far you can get.'

"Well, it's a corny story," she said. "I'll cut it as short as I can. Of course I was a natural at it, as he had suspected I would be. He was a big computer tycoon, almost unbeknownst to me. All I had known for sure was that he was rich. He gave me the whipping that night, but then he ended the term of service early, handed me a couple of pair of jeans and T-shirts, and hired me as a trainee."

"One more popular fantasy come true," I laughed. "But you came back here. How did that happen?"

"Well, that part's more interesting," she answered. "That's where your friend Kate Clarke comes in."

"My friend?" I was surprised, almost spilling my coffee. The meal was ending spectacularly, with coffee, brandy, fruit, cheeses, and crème brulée.

"Well, I guess not your friend," she agreed. "Your friend's friend. And I guess you don't know that you've got a note from her in your file."

There were even fancy cigarettes, Players. She lit one for each of us. "It's not any kind of rave recommendation, you know. But then, she's not given to raving. As I'd expect her to, she describes you quite accurately. She says you have immense potential and somewhat spotty training, and that anybody taking you on should be willing to take on the responsibilities that combination entails. Still, just having the letter there calls attention to you."

How odd, I thought. Anybody reading that letter who knew Jonathan and Kate—and there would definitely be people who did—would know that the message was about more than me. Why would Kate let all that hang out so publicly, I wondered—the polar struggle between her professionalism and his amateurism, the central fact, perhaps, of an odd, frustrating, enduring, lifelong relationship. Oh come on, Carrie, I thought, if we're talking about public exposure here, we could ask you a few questions yourself. But still, how strange that I would know how to interpret that letter, when Margot, for all her vast cool, did not. I turned back to what she was saying.

"Well, my ex-master got to know Kate. I had been the first slave he'd owned, and he felt chagrined that he'd tried so hard to chose somebody for his body and had wound up picking a programmer. He's a hiring genius—I mean, he's known for that—but he didn't want to be doing it all the damn time. So after my period of service was up he didn't go to any more auctions. He started going to Kate's place in Napa, and he took me a few times. I don't suppose you've ever been there?"

"I've only heard about it."

"Well, I'm sure you'll get to go sometime, in some, uh, capacity. It's, it's…delicious. That's the only word I can think of for it. Chez Panisse for sex. I'm glad I got taken there, because I couldn't possibly have afforded what it costs. But what a terrific present. I was at loose ends sexually. I knew what I liked, but I didn't have the time or the energy to get it. That's what's so wonderful about Kate. If you know exactly what you want, she can make it happen for you. You get to know her, too—or she gets to know you, in any case. And one day she and I were both griping about the old-fashioned retro or militaristic trappings that S/M insists on adopting.

"'I can see,' she was saying, 'that period decor is attractive. I have no problem with that. But it can't be the only backdrop for the assertion of power. After all, power gets asserted every day in this world.'

"Well, I started to talk about computers and control and she became fascinated, and one thing led to another, and here I am. Kate got me this job. She knows everybody in this little universe. And it works well for me. I like to create environments that delineate power. You recognized that, didn't you?"

"Yes, I did," I said, "but I'm surprised, now that I think about it. I mean, shouldn't you be doing stuff like VR? Or uh, you know, what do they call it, teledildonics?"

"Oh, please," she said, "helmets and suits with wires in the crotch? Why, is that what turns you on? Of course it isn't. What gets to me—and you—is power, coercive power. Force, directed. I make you do something, go somewhere, be as I wish. You, your flesh, your *prana*. And what I especially like, what has always fascinated me, is making you work at it. I love the fact that you get around here on your own, that you deliver yourself to me, that it is always a stretch, an effort of will and intelligence, to become an object.

"And it's not just one on one, you and me. It's you and all those other slaves, and it's staff and buyers. It's a world, it moves. Power is exercised, but power relations are enacted. I model the form, you reproduce it, in your actions and in your desires. I mean, that's why computers are sexy, isn't it, because they're such sophisticated modeling tools—they inscribe the invisible, inexorable paths of power and energy flow just as surely as Paul's beating marked your lovely ass."

"I understand," I said. "I think I probably even agree with you. But maybe it's a little more one on one around here than you think. Because I immediately recognized you, your hands and your intellect, as the creator of this system. When that ape Karl was screwing me up the ass, what made it bearable was my thinking, my repeating to myself, 'It's Margot, Margot, who's created this pain and humiliation for me.'"

She was silent for a moment. "Oh dear, that's not what I had intended. At least, I don't think so. And it's certainly not what they're paying me for. But I did enjoy hearing you say it. You felt him up your ass and you thought about me?"

I nodded and then stared off into space. We were both gripping our ends of the table, as though it were some kind of Ouija board that would tell us an answer we needed to know. She regained her cool first.

"Well, this job is good, anyhow, and sexually it works out about as well as anything would, given that I often work twenty-hour days. Still..." she looked at me for a long moment. "I do have fantasies."

"For example," I said.

"Oh, well, for example, if I had an extra hundred thou or so, maybe I'd buy you tomorrow," she began.

I started to breath more shallowly.

"I'd take you home," she said, "and I'd beat you every day for weeks, a little more every day. I'd beat you and then I'd fuck you and then you'd make me come with your mouth. And you'd wait for it. You'd be all alone on your knees, chained to the bedpost, waiting for the sound of my footsteps.

"I'd use a long, braided whip, and I'd hang it on the bedroom wall. Sometimes you'd just stare at it for an hour or so, trembling. And sometimes you'd lose yourself and your sense of time and place in reveries about me.

"You know how busy my schedule is, how I work around the clock, I nap on that couch when I absolutely have to. So I could arrive at any time. Sometimes you prick up

183

your ears, get all wet and excited thinking you hear my footsteps, and it's only a servant with your food.

"Or sometimes I am simply too busy to come that day and must send a servant to beat you instead. You have learned to contain your disappointment, and you know that you must obey the servant in every way.

"When I do come, I make you beg for everything, even the beating. You need to be eloquent, to persuade me why I should tax myself, why you need it, how much good it will do you.

"You are very articulate, perhaps too much so. I'd make you put all that verbal inventiveness to good use."

I gripped the edges of my chair. I hadn't had caffeine or alcohol in days, and I hardly ever smoked. So all the potent legal drugs I'd just ingested were combining to make my head swim, and my cunt was wet and burning. She stood up, wheeled the table away, and looked down at me.

"Take your clothes off, Carrie," she said.

"I thought," I stammered, even as I started to unbutton the dress, "that you had this, uh, ritual here ..."

"Shut up," she snapped, "unless you want another spanking."

I stood up and took off all the clothes, slowing down a little as I took off the underwear. She'd gotten it for me, I thought, so maybe she'd want to see it a little. And she did smile a bit at that point. But then I hurried along. No point pushing my luck.

"Kneel in front of the couch," she continued, when I was naked. "Back to the couch, facing me. And you can look at me."

"Yes, Mistress," I said, without even thinking too much about it. "Thank you, Mistress."

"Good girl," she said, and took off her silk shirt. Her breasts were small and round, with very dark nipples. They were beautiful under her wide shoulders. She walked over to her desk and picked up a manila envelope.

"I want you to see how your photographs turned out," she said, and handed me two prints. Then she sat behind me on the couch, her legs straddling me, her hands on my breasts, her breasts touching my shoulders. "Do you like them?" she asked close to my ear. "Tell the truth, slave."

I figured I'd better. "No, Mistress," I said.

She squeezed my breasts painfully, "And why not?"

The pictures were very careful, very documentary jobs. She had been right the other day; Paul did good work. The light was harsh; the general effect was of truth-telling. Something about the marks on my ass, the shadows under my eyes, the pallor of my skin. Nobody was being flattered, the pictures said, but this was itself a form of flattery. And if the viewers were not being flattered, they were certainly being asked to participate, if only imaginatively.

"Here," the pictures seemed to say, "this is for you, if you want it. She will receive whatever you care to give: caresses, thrusts of your hand or cock, blows. It's up to you. Interested?"

I was scared to see how I had posed for the pictures. In the front view, I thrust my pelvis out a little, as though I were offering guests something to eat. I looked shocked and a little outraged, but I held the pose anyway. Even in the back view, smarting and still sobbing from a beating, I held myself up. I was surprised at how firmly my feet were planted on the floor. I had remembered dangling from my suspended wrists, but in fact the pose was much more provocative. I couldn't deny it; without even realizing it, I had complied with Paul and Margot. I was showing off the bruises. I was displaying myself for buyers. I looked proud to be able to receive pain.

I was showing myself to whomever and whatever, to strangers, who could do anything they wanted to me; I was offering myself to the highest bidder.

"Why not, slave?" she asked again, this time twisting my nipples and making me gasp.

"They frighten me, Mistress," I temporized. I knew she'd insist on hearing me more. "I...I look willing to be hurt," I mumbled.

"And?" she insisted.

"I look available to everybody," I said sadly. "And proud of it."

"These are wonderful pictures," she said, moving one of her hands in slow circles down to my belly. "Right now, in various expensive hotels and *pieds-à-terre* in this city, there are dozens of people looking at these pictures. They are considering whether they would like to fuck you, whether they would like to hurt you, whether you could be led and trained and forced to become what they want. You look like...new red wine. Beaujolais Nouveau. The depth is still developing, but the sweetness caresses the tongue and touches the heart. Not everyone wants it, but it is a unique pleasure."

Her hand had reached the opening of my vagina. Her fingers were slowly searching their way around. I wanted to drop the pictures, but I was afraid to. I just kept staring at myself and feeling her. She'd reached my clitoris. She was in no hurry. I heard myself moaning. I dropped the pictures and leaned into her leather-clad thighs, her bare breasts, her hair, her mouth on my neck. And then she stopped.

Lithely, she swung a leg over me and stood up. She turned to face me.

"I would whip you right now if I could," she said. "I'd love to see you trembling and weeping under me. But I can't. We'll manage, though."

She went to a drawer and pulled out some black leather, and something else. A harness for me? No, a harness for her, I realized hazily, as I watched her fit the big dildo into place. It was a heavy clear plastic—virtual phallus, I couldn't help thinking. She pulled some zippers on her leather pants, and they fell away from her lean belly, though they stayed around her legs like a second skin. And then she quickly strapped on the harness while I looked at her in awe. Bright skin against black leather, shiny transparent up-curving member, insolent smile, clouded, intense eyes.

I was still kneeling in front of the couch. She nudged the dildo into my mouth, deep, deep, deep, and then she pulled out and pulled me to my feet. She lay down on the couch and pulled me into a straddle on top of her, the dildo deep in my cunt, making me groan as I raised and lowered myself on her. Her fingernails played with my nipples. She moved her hips subtly, suavely. Her hands were on my ass now, squeezing my flesh and moving me with her. And I followed her blindly, seeing her face through a haze of pleasure, the hard dildo probing deep inside me, my groans louder and louder, cresting to a howling orgasm.

She didn't let me recover very long. Quickly, she pushed me off her and forced me down to my hands and knees. She took off the harness and pulled my mouth down on her. I licked, I sucked, I nibbled. I wanted to do everything she might possibly want. I wanted to hear her cry out. I succeeded. She took her hands off my head and stroked my back, my ass. I lay with my head in her lap.

187

I heard a low laugh. She raised my head and kissed me a long time on the lips. I held her tightly.

"Do you think," I murmured, "that I'll ever see you again, after tomorrow?"

She nibbled at my neck a little more before she answered.

"Well," she said, "I do have some influence. I don't use it much, but I suppose that makes it more valuable. So if what I think is going to happen happens…well, yes, maybe you will see me again. But only after you've been worked so rigorously that you will have almost forgotten me."

I looked at her imploringly.

"No," she said, "I'm not telling you a word more."

I sighed, though of course I wasn't surprised.

"But I won't forget you," I said, kissing her hand.

"You won't forget me, what?" she asked sternly.

"I won't forget you, Mistress," I said meekly, dropping my eyes. End of idyll.

I didn't want to move, but she got up and started searching around for her shirt. When she'd gotten it sloppily buttoned up, she walked to her desk and found my bracelet. I was still on my knees in front of the couch, my head resting on my arms, but I turned and straightened into a position of attention, raising my arm passively to let her buckle on the bracelet.

"Get up," she said, and when I did she led me to the door.

"If you've forgotten how to get back to your room," she said, "the Argus will help you, of course."

Of course. And just then, as she opened the door, the bracelet prickled.

"You're going to be very tired tomorrow morning," she said, pushing me gently into the hall. "All the other slaves have had their regular tofu dinners and special baths and massages. Except, of course, for that crazy boy with the ponytail, who's probably still down in the kitchen, servicing every woman who works there." She chuckled and kissed me on the forehead. I was too tired and satiated to be anything but amused as well.

"Sleep well, Carrie," she said, and closed her door. As I waved my bracelet over the Argus, trying my groggy, confused best to make sense of the diagram that appeared on the screen, I heard the keys at her keyboard clicking fiercely away.

CHAPTER VII

What Happens Next?

I was considerably less amused the next morning, if it was morning at all when the maid woke me up. It was dark outside, and I was a mess. The maid gave me a nice bath and a brief massage, which helped somewhat. I guess she was catching me up with last night. I grimaced ruefully when I remembered how readily I'd bought Margot's story. Last supper. Right. Everybody gets his or her favorite food. We've got salmon for Carrie, and then, let's see…how about jelly beans for Tommy, colored eggs for Sister Sue? Still, it was a nice memory and what had I lost? Some sleep was really all. Better, I supposed, to be rushing through these preparations than have all the time in the world to be scared to death of what the day would hold.

And of course, as soon as I thought about being scared to death, I realized that scared to death was exactly what I was. I mean, it had been one thing to have Jonathan—who, when you got right down to it, was a composite of crushes I'd had throughout my life—pick me up at a party. It would be quite another to surrender my body and will—for a year—to anybody, anybody at all who had the bucks. Could be somebody really gross. Could be somebody dumb. Could be somebody I didn't—underneath it all—actually like. I was choosing to put myself in about the most choiceless situation I could imagine.

What puzzled me, when I looked at it that way, was why I wasn't more frightened still, why I was still willing to go through with it, why so many of my nerve endings were eager, awake, and alert.

But they were. I lapped up the rice gruel eagerly, I relaxed into whatever the maid wanted to do with my body, cleaning me up, making up my face, attaching small placards with the number 14 to the rings, front and back, of my collar, locking a cold, narrow, iron cuff around my left ankle, and then leaving me alone in my room.

The bracelet buzzed soon after, and I walked out into the corridor. And for the first time, I wasn't just tracing my own solitary path through that place. Rather, there was a whole tide of us, naked, tits and cocks bouncing, numbers hanging from our collars, terrified yet resolute expressions on our faces, a parade of us walking the now-familiar route toward the Garden.

When I got there, a security guard, dressed in a spiffy uniform and holding a walkie-talkie, took off the bracelet, checked my number, and moved me into the quickly forming line of slaves. It was all going along so quickly and fluidly that I didn't really have time to think. As I approached the door, I could see into the Garden, which was full of beautifully dressed buyers and marvelously decorated with bright silk tents and banners, in the colors of a medieval book of hours. A stage had been erected in the center, and there were pedestals to the side of it, with some slaves already standing on them.

The guard at the door whispered in the ear of the slave at the front of the line—all I could really see was fine straight ash blond hair down to her ass and long elegant legs. Then a trumpet sounded, and he smacked her hard on the ass. She ran out to the area in front of the stage, where another guard was standing, and turned, knelt, and kissed the ground in the direction of the crowd of buyers while an announcer up on a stage read off her number and the page of the catalog where you could read more about her. Then a guard took hold of her wrist and led her to a pedestal. And by that time, the next slave was being smacked and running...so gracefully, how would I ever...? And then I was next.

I hardly heard the instructions whispered in my ear, but it seemed like there were no surprises, nothing I hadn't already learned by watching. It was just that I couldn't, couldn't possibly — there were too many people out there, it was all a terrible mistake, I'd just slink back to my room and work it all out later, and...I heard the sharp sound of the smack on my ass more than I felt it, and then I was running, feeling nothing but the smoothness of the cold tiles under my feet and about a thousand knowing sophisticated eyes on my body. There's the guard. Stop. Turn. Kneel and kiss the ground. He knows where to take me, I just have to follow him, to that pedestal over there, past that group of people watching so intently. I saw Chloe, laughing up at Francis and André. Some nasty Eurotrash boys who'd come to my room one morning and made a little gauntlet of cocks for me to suck and who seemed to be happily reminiscing about it now. I saw Margot, in the distance, her brow furrowed, keeping track of the proceedings like an orchestra conductor with the whole score of the symphony in his head. Jonathan, looking pale, as though he'd just finished a workaholic binge, watching me intensely and dragging deeply on a cigarette. And Kate Clarke, briskly taking Jonathan's arm and threading their way back through the crowd.

And then the guard was attaching a long chain attached to the pedestal to the iron cuff on my ankle. "Head up," he muttered to me. "Eyes down. And breathe."

It was good advice, the breathing part, I realized, especially after all the slaves had run to their pedestals, and there was one last hour when the buyers could check us over. There were just so many eyes on me, and fingers, nudges, pokes, laughs, and comments. I preferred it when the comments were in languages I couldn't understand. Arabic, I guessed. Japanese. I kept my eyes down. And breathed. And tried not to concentrate on anybody as an individual, but as an element in the swirling, hydra-headed, shiva-handed, multicolored, polyglot, gorgeously dressed crowd.

So I was surprised when there was a momentary parting of the crowd around me. I looked up, just a little, enough to see a by-now-familiar flash of dark, gray-tinted glasses. And then quickly down, my stunned brain stupidly registering that no director of security anywhere could afford shoes as expensive as the ones I was looking down at. I felt cool, dry fingers parting my ass as if it were a tangerine.

"Look, Stefan," I heard, in precise, oddly unaccented but clearly foreign English. "It's been the same all week, the expression on her face. She can't help it, it breaks through all the mediocre training she's had. That pure passion for obedience. What do you think?"

The other voice was not as clear, but anyway it was hard for me to hear right then, hard for me to perceive anything except my response to the fingers up me. I wanted those fingers to force me to do something—something difficult and painful, something I had never done before but would try *so* hard to do, if he'd just keep touching me. And then I realized

193

where we were and how close I was to losing it altogether, and all I wanted was not to come, not to lose myself in trembling, dissolving sobs and cries. My belly did start to tremble, which he noticed, and he stroked it a little, mercifully taking his other fingers out of me.

"She has a great, great deal to learn," he said softly to Stefan, whom I perceived through my downcast eyes as a blurry set of black snakeskin cowboy boots, "but still, I think she and I understand each other, don't you?"

Soon after, they led me to the big pink-and-blue silk tent behind the stage, to prepare for the actual bidding. A big guy in a dumb-looking leather outfit—George, I guessed—silently gagged me, slung me over his knee, and, quite unemotionally, gave me the most total spanking of my life. I was a mess after it, in fact, heaving and sobbing, and needed to be cleaned up and comforted, which he also did, quite competently, stroking my forehead, kissing my cheek. Just as I was beginning to feel all right though—not my ass, but the rest of me—with practically no warning I was dragged out to the stage. Just barely, I remembered the instructions I'd gotten before the spanking, dropping to my knees and kissing the ground in front of the auctioneer. He got the audience's attention by pretending to be surprised by my Schiaparelli pink ass, and had me display it to them at some length. He asked me if it hurt, and when I said, "Yes, Master," he pinched it very hard. I couldn't help the few tears that ran down my cheeks, but I was proud that I didn't sob or anything, and I was glad that some scattered applause seemed to acknowledge that. Again, I remembered to breathe.

Mercifully, they started the bidding after that, with the auctioneer holding me tightly by the arm, moving me around a bit when he felt it was going a little slowly, to show off different parts of my body or to elaborate on my few other salable points—the letter from Kate Clarke, my ability to take punishment in French. There were bright lights trained at the stage, so I couldn't see the bidders. I heard a female voice that I recognized as Kate Clarke's, but I was sure that she wasn't seriously bidding, just teasing Jonathan by pretending to be, and perhaps boosting his ego by helping to up my price a little. I was just a little disappointed, I realized, that she wasn't bidding for real.

Mostly, though, I think I was pretty numbed by it all—spanking, the exposure, that amazing wrenching feeling when I'd been examined by that last buyer, and the realization that this big-budget Technicolor extravaganza of a scene and ritual would have real consequences. A year of my life was being decided here. All I could do was wait and wonder what in the world I'd gotten myself into. The only specific thing I had to go on was the auctioneer's final rap of the gavel and cry, "Sold. To Mr. Constant for one year at $92,500."

Then they took off the iron cuff and the collar with the number 14 placards, led me into a little tent somewhat back from the stage, and told me to get ready. A young man dressed in black, with a short ponytail and those black cowboy boots, came in a few minutes later, and told me that he was Stefan, Mr. Constant's secretary. He seemed severe but reasonably cordial.

"On your knees," he said. "Now, you'll learn everything in due course, but a little information before we leave here, just to give you something to go on. Mr. Constant lives some of the time on a Greek island and some of the time in Manhattan. He divides his time between taking care of his money—he's got a very devoted staff that helps him—and being very very strict with his slaves—that's you, now, of course, and a boy named Tony. Oh, and there's also a trainer for you and Tony, mostly for when we're busy or away."

We? I wondered. What else does the devoted staff get to do? This one had a pretty mouth.

He caught my glance and said "Watch it." Then he continued, "Mr. Constant is very meticulous, but he's also very fair; he's generous, too. He's rather creative as well, and he likes a bargain, which is why it was fun to buy you. And once in a while he gives a fabulous party. You could have done a lot worse. Still, there will be what I believe they call a learning curve...."

I nodded. Of course there would be a learning curve.

Stefan gave me some high black boots to put on and lace up. As I was doing that, he reached into his pocket and handed me an envelope. I opened it and found this note.

Dear Carrie,

You will continue brave and beautiful, I know. In a year, you'll be much more so than you are now. I sold you at this auction because I wanted to see if I—and you—could pull it off. But I also did it because if I hadn't done it, I would have wanted to call the whole game off and see if we could become friends. Or lovers. Or something. Go to the movies together and see if we liked the same ones. I still want to and this is both surprising and disturbing. I'll be at the Place d'Horloge in Avignon next

March 15. That's two weeks after your term of service ends. Come if you want to. I'll know you by the glasses and the clunky shoes. You can pay for your own dinner. Hell, Constant will invest your money so well that you can pay for mine, too.
Salut, J.

P.S. I read *Mirrorshades* after you were gone. It's an interesting book, isn't it, and I thought you'd probably want to finish it, so I sent it along. You'll get it when you get where you're going. They let you have books, you know, for periodic R&R.

I wanted to stamp my foot, in its stiff new boot, with rage. Selfish, spoiled, uncool, I thought. Unfair. Romantic, amateurish, I rather surprised myself by thinking, as well. Shit, I thought, I've just gone through all this and this is the moment he picks for his big, coy, rueful, reluctant male confession. He'd promised to give me a narrative in which to enact my fantasies—who would have thought that it would turn out to be a goddamn Harlequin Romance.

And then the humor of the situation sank in. Oh, Jonathan, I thought, I've heard about this male fear of commitment, but you certainly went to some ridiculous lengths, just to avoid asking me to a movie. Not to speak of taking me out to dinner—I giggled a little when I realized how deftly Margot had managed that one, under the least promising of circumstances. I crumbled the letter to throw it away, but then changed my mind. Very slowly, I smoothed it out. They'd given me a metal strongbox for papers that I wouldn't be needing for the year. My birth certificate, driver's license, checkbook, diploma. That silly little contract Jonathan had insisted on, ensuring that I couldn't get at my $654 until my term of service was up. Pictures of Stuart and me, taken in one of those booths at Woolworth's, grinning and mugging in four frames. Stuart would want to see the letter, I thought as I laid it on top of the pile and closed the box. Anyway, I would be glad to get the chance to finish *Mirrorshades*. And I couldn't help wondering which of the stories he'd liked best, damn him.

Stefan put the box in his briefcase. I could see my file in there too. Then he wrapped me in a rough black cloak and led me out of the Garden, down another corridor, and out of the building. There was a limo parked at the door, and Mr. Constant was sitting inside. I climbed in next to him and waited to be told how to greet him.